Peter
Treegate's
War

Ariel Books by Leonard Wibberley

Fiction

PETER TREEGATE'S WAR
JOHN TREEGATE'S MUSKET
KEVIN O'CONNOR AND THE LIGHT BRIGADE
THE WOUND OF PETER WAYNE
DEADMEN'S CAVE
THE SECRET OF THE HAWK
THE KING'S BEARD

Non-fiction

WES POWELL, CONQUEROR OF THE GRAND CANYON
JOHN BARRY, FATHER OF THE NAVY
THE LIFE OF WINSTON CHURCHILL
THE EPICS OF EVEREST
THE CORONATION BOOK

Peter Treegate's War

by

LEONARD WIBBERLEY

ARIEL BOOKS

FARRAR, STRAUS AND CUDAHY • NEW YORK

Ariel Books is a division of Farrar, Straus and
Cudahy, Inc. Published simultaneously in
Canada by Ambassador Books, Ltd., Toronto.

Manufactured in the U.S.A. by H. Wolff

Peter
Treegate's
War

1

In the year 1775, the day being the 17th of June, I Peter Treegate, sixteen, was standing behind breastworks on the flank of a hill across the Charles River from the city of Boston. The day was as pleasant as could be wished for, and it struck me as strange, with the sound of larks in my ears and the sun turning the grass to a pale gold, that I was there to kill men—as many men as I could before I was perhaps killed myself.

I was not alone in the trench on Breed's Hill. Beside

me to my left was the Maclaren of Spey, my foster father, and on my right, my true father, John Treegate. On either side of us, along the line of the trench which we had put up the night before, were several hundred more men, all of them armed, and all members of various militia companies of the New England colonies. We were waiting for the redcoats, who were landing on the coastline at the foot of the hill, to form their battle line and charge.

The Maclaren of Spey was short and dark-haired and dressed in deerskins. He had a belt around his waist with a tomahawk and hunting knife thrust in it, and hanging from the belt a powder horn and a bag of bullets. He watched the redcoats form into platoons and companies and regiments coolly and with contempt.

"They'll be an oor yet," he said in the thick accent of the Scottish Highlands. "They took an oor and a half at Drummossie Muir."

"Half an hour at Abraham Heights," said my father, looking over at the Maclaren. "I was fighting with them then. With this same musket. I am not happy that I must fight against them now."

"Make up yir mind whose side ye're on," said the Maclaren, spitefully.

"I have," said my father coolly. "That is why I am here and why my son is here."

"He is here to avenge Drummossie Muir," said the Maclaren.

"He is here to fight against tyranny," said my father.

"What does it matter so long as I fight?" I said to put an end to the bickering between these two men, who both loved me and hated each other.

It is necessary to explain this hatred between my father and my foster father, the Maclaren of Spey. It was a matter quite as much of history as of personal relationship. No doubt there have been many similar hatreds between men who, had they not been caught up in history, might have been good friends.

The Maclaren of Spey was a Scotsman who had once been chief of a small clan in the Highlands of his own country. He wore even now on his deerskin jacket a tara brooch with a peculiarly cut stone set in it which marked his position as the chief of the clan of Maclaren. Under the brooch was a piece of tartan, also belonging to his clan. His people had been killed during or after the Battle of Culloden (which he called Drummossie Muir), fought in Scotland in 1745 between the Scots and the English. He had had three sons (one an infant of a few months), a wife, and a clan of three hundred of his kin. All but himself had been killed. He had managed to escape to the American colonies and penetrated to the Carolina backwoods.

My father had no such exciting background. He had been a quiet, respected merchant of Boston, intensely loyal to King George, and had served in the English Army during the French and Indian Wars. Indeed, he had taken part in the Battle of Abraham Heights as a volunteer with the English forces, and the Tower musket he now held in his hands, he had used on that day.

These two men, of such varied backgrounds, would never have met, but for me.

When I was nine years of age my father had gone to London at his own expense, in an effort to reconcile the growing differences between the Mother Country and the colonies in America.

While he was away, I had been entrusted, as an apprentice, to a barrelmaker of Boston. But as the result of the bullying of a fellow apprentice I had fled Boston on a ship, been shipwrecked, and then picked up on the shores of Carolina by the Maclaren of Spey. At that time I could not remember who I was.

The Maclaren of Spey had taken me to his cabin, which was a week's march into the Carolina wilderness, and brought me up as his own son. It was only recently that my memory had returned, and I had rejoined my father in Boston in time for the battle which we now awaited.

I had then been brought up in Carolina as a frontiersman and wore the same deerskins as the Maclaren. I was a better shot than he, but it was he who had taught me to shoot. He could still outwrestle me because he knew more tricks. But I was nearly six feet and still growing. I hated the British—partly because of the Maclaren and what he had suffered at their hands, partly because of what I had seen of their behavior in the colonies.

So I stood between these two men—the Maclaren, who fought for Scotland and vengeance, my father, still something of a stranger to me, who fought for freedom from tyranny.

I wondered, watching the redcoats form below, which of the two was the most important to me. In short, to whom was I most attached—the Maclaren of Spey, who had brought me up and saved my life, or John Treegate, my father, whom I hardly knew?

I looked at my father for a moment as he stood beside me. His white wig had a smear of dirt on it from the digging we had done during the night putting up the trenches in which we now stood. Yet it had an air of neatness. His clothes were of brown worsted—the suit of a merchant to be worn in the countinghouse. He had on a pair of good shoes with large French buckles, and indeed his whole costume contrasted strongly with the deerskins which I and the Maclaren wore. With five minutes to make his toilet, he would be ready for any business appointment, and yet here he stood bravely with his musket before him, awaiting battle. He showed no sign of fear.

On the shore at the foot of the hill below us two long parallels of soldiers had now formed; their crossed bandoliers showed plainly against their scarlet tunics, and their heavy knapsacks were hoisted up above their shoulders as a frame for their heads.

Then came the command, "Fix bayonets." We heard it quite clearly in our trenches, and I felt a tightening of my stomach muscles as the bayonets were pulled from their scabbards and put with a click on the muskets.

A man in a uniform of red and gold rode to the front of the British line and cantered along it. When he had got to the end he turned his horse to face us, drew his sword, and shouted in a high-pitched voice, "The line will advance upon the enemies' works." Then there was a crash of drums and a screaming of fifes, and the two lines of redcoats, one behind the other, stepped off coming up the hill toward us, and the battle for which we had waited so long commenced.

The redcoats advanced slowly and deliberately. They came to a low fence and rolled over this like ants and re-formed their line on the other side and so came on. Somebody in the trenches near me said in a shaky voice, "May God be with us," and certainly it was enough to unnerve any man to see the precision with which the British came up the hill, like a tide which could not be resisted.

"Steady now," someone called. "Hold your fire and aim low." These words were passed along among us, from one man to his neighbor, half in a whisper, as if they contained in themselves some secret formula for salvation.

The British came nearer and nearer until it was possible to pick out details of uniforms, and we, in the trenches behind the breastwork, felt tense like men holding their breath and uncertain whether they can hold it a moment longer. Still we held our fire.

I recall the sounds of those moments as the British came toward us. There was first the thump of their feet on the ground, then the swish of the long grass against their gaiters, then the beat of the drums marking the time for the marching infantry, and then, much closer to me, the hard short breathing of the men around.

The advancing infantry now halted, splendid against the knee-deep grass. The drums stopped their steady dull beat. The general officer in front on his horse sat immobile, his curved cavalry sword unsheathed and raised above his head. From company to company of the men behind him sped the order:

"Ready!"

Down came the shouldered muskets, to be held across the chest.

"Aim!"

And the muskets were brought into the firing position.

"Fire!"

Swiftly the two lines disappeared from our view in a cloud of white smoke, which for a second was stitched with dagger-shaped points of yellow flame.

A storm of bullets smacked into the breastwork before us, so that it looked as if the front of the redoubt had exploded and the earth from it was flung in a curiously flat cloud up in the air. Then smoke and earth cleared, and when it did we saw the lines of the British still advancing, this time with their bayonets at the ready.

The Maclaren of Spey jumped to the top of the breastwork beside me in plain view of the enemy and shook a knotted fist at them.

"Drummossie Muir," he shouted. "Thirty years I've

waited." He brought up his long rifle, took aim at an officer before one of the companies, and pressed the trigger. The officer crumbled to his knees and fell, and his men, without a pause, without breaking line, stepped over him and kept on coming.

The shot of the Maclaren of Spey was the signal for the opening of fire from the breastworks, which up to this time had remained ominously quiet. We all fired, some hastily, some more leisurely. For myself, trained by the Maclaren, I picked a target and toppled a big grenadier with my first ball.

The whole top of the breastwork around me exploded with firing, which was taken up along the line of a rail fence, stuffed with haybales and turfs, to our left and rear.

The range was a little over a hundred paces, and the fire was not over in one swift salvo as had been the case with the British. It started with a few irregular discharges, increased in intensity, reached a tremendous crescendo which was sustained for perhaps two minutes, and then gradually diminished until it was once again possible to distinguish the noise of individual rifles or muskets.

I remember that I was able, in the fusillade, to load and fire four times, so that I reckoned that the discharge from the breastwork must have lasted at least six minutes. But finally the firing died away and the thick white smoke which had arisen from it drifted slowly off, clinging to the tops of the long grass.

Peering through this smoke before it was well

cleared, I saw here and there a glimpse of red, a few snatches of color, though I could not, for a while, make out the complete form of a single man. It occurred to me that the British were still coming on, this time with their bayonets, so I put down my rifle and took my tomahawk from my belt, and got up on the parapet where I could be free of others around me and so could use the tomahawk more effectively.

The Maclaren pulled out his hunting knife, a broad eight-inch blade, and joined me, and glancing back I saw my father now held in his hand a sword.

Then a little flurry of wind blew the remaining smoke away, and I stared down the slope of the hill, scarcely believing what I saw. The slope was for a distance of a hundred yards deep-carpeted with dead or dying red-coats.

They lay indeed in windrows as if cut down by a scythe. Their breeches and garters were blotched with blood, and there were only a few on their feet among them. These looked in amazement at their fallen comrades and at each other, but made no other move. Then there was a shout from over to the left of "Withdraw in good order and re-form," and the drums beat the retreat.

The men who had survived our fire turned and walked as slowly down the hill as they had come up it, and not a shot was fired at them as they went, so surprised were we at the destruction we had wrought.

"They're beaten," someone shouted. "We've driven them off."

The shout broke a spell of silence and of wonder which had settled on us, and we now began to cheer. We cheered again and again until we were hoarse, and some started to climb out of the entrenchment and run to the rear to spread the good news.

"Back!" shouted my father, seeing this. "Back, I say! They will come again."

"Not after we gave them such a bloody welcome the first time," said a man whom I later discovered was a farmer from Medford. "They've had their rations for the day."

"Ye're plain daft, man," shouted the Maclaren. "They'll come again and again. I know them well. And what we maun do is save our powder, or we will lose all."

"They won't come back," said the farmer. "Half of them are lying out there now. They've had a bellyful."

"Look," shouted my father. "They're re-forming already."

It was true. At the foot of the hill by the shore, the red lines were being drawn up once more. Again there was no hurry about it. All was done with leisure. The men dressed on each other in companies and in regiments, but the regiments were smaller now. A few more marines were landed from some of the vessels in the harbor, and then, to a ruffle of drums and a shrilling of pipes, the red tide flowed again slowly up the hill.

"The mixture as before," said my father to me. He did not laugh or smile as he said this, but spoke gravely.

"Do you think we can turn them again?" I asked.

"While we have powder," said my father. "I have enough for half a dozen rounds and no more."

The Maclaren of Spey was on the top of the parapet near me, haranguing the men of his company. When he was excited he spoke in a mixture of Scots dialect and Gaelic, so that the men had some difficulty in understanding what he was saying, though I could follow him well enough.

He was telling them not to throw away their powder, but once more to fire only when the redcoats were nearly upon us. He said he would stand on the breastwork and pick off officers of the companies as they came up the hill. His men were to hand loaded muskets to him while he did this.

"The range is short," he cried. "Dinna use more powder than is needed tae send a ball two hundred yards. And dinna spill any like daft, frightened wimmen." Since I was as good a marksman as he, I decided to join him on the breastwork and pick off officers as well.

I climbed up and watched the approach of the lines of infantry.

"Officers only," said the Maclaren, when we were ready. He bent down, picked up a handful of dust from the top of the breastwork and let it fall from his fingers, judging the wind by the way it was dispersed. I watched him do this. I was using a one-ounce ball and decided that two inches to the left at three hundred yards would be right on the target.

"I'll take yon turkey cock wi' the bonnie big hat," said the Maclaren, and brought his rifle up. There was a report, and the officer flung backward on the ground. For myself I picked a major of the marines and tumbled him with a round through the head. I was used to this kind of work, fighting and hunting, in the Carolina wilds, and felt cool and relaxed as I selected my targets, took aim, and fired.

We picked off several officers between us, the loaded muskets being passed up to us as arranged, and at each shot the men behind us cheered. Then several British grenadiers detached themselves from the advancing lines and opened fire on us. The Maclaren spun around with a ball through his arm, and another whipped through my loose deerskin jacket.

"Get down," my father shouted, pulling at my leggings.

I glanced at the Maclaren of Spey, who was in the trench. There was a dark blotch on his deerskin on the left arm near the shoulder.

"Are you badly hurt?" I asked, still standing on the breastwork.

" 'Twill heal better if ye get one more for me," said the Maclaren. I turned with my rifle and a bullet struck the butt, nearly knocking me off balance. But I brought the piece up to my shoulder and fired, and one of the grenadiers toppled.

Then I got down behind the entrenchment, and, ignoring the approach of the enemy, took my hunting knife and opened the sleeve of the Maclaren's deerskin jacket, slitting it along the hem so as not to spoil the skin. The ball had passed through the muscles of the upper arm, severing a vein so that there was a great amount of blood.

"Get back tae yir worrk," said the Maclaren roughly, and pushed me away with his good arm. He was a savage man, always impatient of tenderness, but I knew how to handle him from experience. There were torn fringes of leather on the sleeve of his deerskin, not for decoration but for use. I cut off several of these, and, with them, bound his sleeve around his wound to serve as a temporary dressing, and then returned to the breastwork. He did not thank me.

"You love him deeply," said my father. There was a trace of hurt in his voice.

I did not reply, but, looking at the approaching red-coats, said, "Two hundred paces. They will fire soon."

As if this had been an order, the British lines now stopped, fired, as they had done before, their bullets being uselessly spent on the breastwork, and then came on again through their own battle smoke.

Once more we opened fire from our trench, producing the same long-drawn volley rising to its crescendo and diminishing and occupying perhaps as much as six or seven minutes. When the smoke had cleared away the carnage was even worse than it was before.

The dead and wounded of the British lay tumbled on top of each other, some face down, some on their backs, some on hands and knees, and others sitting in the trampled grass. Because of their heavy knapsacks many of them had toppled over on their backs, and the wounded lay staring at the sky. They were anchored to the ground by the weight of their packs, and many of them died in that position.

Some less seriously hurt managed to unbuckle the webbing which fastened their heavy kit to them, and, thus freed, crawled on hands and knees, or dragged themselves, or hobbled down the hill. Those who had survived came on a few paces—perhaps not more than seven or eight, and again came the shout, "Withdraw in good order and re-form," and the drums beat a retreat for the second time. I was amazed that they showed no panic, and for the first time that day began to feel uneasy. Even their wounded did not scream as I had known the Indians to scream when they were hurt. They just lay there in the grass while the blood ran from their hurts.

This time we in the trench did not cheer. And the farmer from Medford did not ask whether they would come again. He knew that they would, and he took off his powder horn and flung it away grimly and bitterly.

He had no powder left.

2

There was now a desperate search for gunpowder among the men in our trench. Powder became on the moment the most important thing in life; that indeed upon which life would depend. My father and the Maclaren of Spey and the other officers in the redoubt canvassed their men hurriedly on the amount of powder they had left in their pouches or powder horns. My father, knowing that there were some cannon to the rear —half a dozen pieces which could not be brought into action—sent four men back to them to get the gunpowder from the cannon, and these came back with several big cartridges apiece.

The powder was shared around among those who needed it, but it was of coarse grain and not well suited to muskets and rifles. My own powder horn had been half full at the start of the battle. I still had sufficient for perhaps four rounds, but no more. "There's powder to spare out there," I said, pointing to the British dead and wounded on the slope of the hill. I slipped over the earthwork and sped from man to man, relieving each of his pouch, and got half a dozen before returning to the earthwork.

I was just in time in getting back, for the diminished regiments of the British, one half of whose number now lay upon the slopes of the hill, had re-formed and again to the tapping of drums and the shrilling of pipes set out once more up the hill toward us.

I distributed the powder pouches I had collected. For some, however, there was no powder, and these stood helpless in the rear of the redoubt, their muskets useless. A few had thrown away their muskets and armed themselves with the spades and mattocks with which they had built the redoubt, and, thus armed, waited grimly.

Those who had still a shot left lined the front of the redoubt and watched the British advance.

I could see a change now in the British lines. They came on more swiftly than they had before, for they had left behind them the hundred-pound packs which they had carried up the hill on their backs in the two previous charges. Also they did not march with their muskets shouldered but with them across the chest at the "ready." My father noted this too and said to me, "They won't fire this time. They'll come at us with the bayonet."

"Those of them that get through," I replied, eying the riflemen in the breastwork.

"Yes," said my father. "Those of them that get through. But when it comes to close quarters, we haven't a bayonet or a sword to a hundred men."

So we waited as the British came nearer and nearer, the drummers still tapping to mark the time for the men.

When the red lines were within two hundred paces of the redoubt and still had not paused to fire, an uneven crackle of musketry erupted from the breastwork. I think we fired too soon this time, and in any case the fire was not heavy enough. There was not even sufficient smoke from the discharge to obliterate the lines of the advancing British. I saw some of them fall, but the rest stepped over these and came onward, looming larger and seeming more indestructible with each moment.

Then came a shout from the British of "Up and at them," and the redcoats' muskets were brought level so that the bayonets pointed like a hedge of spikes straight at us, and the line broke into a run and stormed up the breastwork. A man does better in hand-to-hand fighting if he has room, so I jumped atop the breastwork with my tomahawk ready and brought down one of the grenadiers as he came at me with his bayonet. An officer swung at me with his sword and I tomahawked him in the arm. He dropped the sword and I picked it up, using it in my left hand. In a moment all became confusion.

A few muskets were discharged which created some smoke, and the dry dust from the entrenchment rose in clouds, so that after a minute or two it was hard to distinguish friend from enemy. Someone caught me in the chest with a clubbed musket and I was thrown backward, head over heels into the trench behind the breastwork. I got to my hands and knees and leaped aside as a redcoat thrust at me with his long bayonet. The bayonet entered the ground, and I flung my weight against the rifle stock, toppling the redcoat over, and finished him with a blow of my tomahawk. Then I heard the Maclaren of Spey shouting from somewhere near me, "Maclaren Abu. Maclaren Abu!" It was only then that I recalled that he was wounded, and I knew he would not shout unless hard-pressed and that he was shouting for me.

I found him fighting with his hunting knife, his back to the rear of the trench. He was so lithe and quick upon his feet that, with their clumsy bayonets on the end of their thirteen-pound muskets, the redcoats around could not get at him. Three of them lay within the circle which he had cut for himself. But his left sleeve was all blood, and his tanned face gray from the loss of it. I jumped out of the trench and got behind and above the Maclaren.

"Up," I shouted, and reached down and grabbed him by the shoulders. I had him out of the trench in a second and flung him, pushing him before me, to the rear, for I knew the trench could not be held any longer. He had gone only a few paces when he stumbled to his knees.

I picked him up, putting him across my shoulders, for I could carry him readily and had done so once before in Carolina when he had broken a leg. In this manner I took him to the rear in the rout that followed the storming of the trench.

There was a narrow neck of land which connected the peninsula on which the battle had taken place with the mainland, and all were now making for this. Some of the officers tried to rally our men on a hill called Bunker Hill to the rear of our old position. I believe the men would have made a stand there if they'd had powder or even bayonets.

But they had nothing with which to defend themselves. And so we stumbled and jostled to the neck of land to find that it was swept with cannon fire from British ships in the water on either side.

The ships were so close in that the smoke from their guns swept over this bridge of land which we must cross to safety, and it was impossible to see more than a few feet ahead. The British were using cannon balls, and that was a mercy. To be sure, men were knocked down all about me, but had the enemy used grape shot

—that is, big musket balls fired out of the cannon—I don't think anyone could have got from the peninsula to the mainland.

How I made it myself I do not know. The Maclaren of Spey said afterward that it was because he had recited the words of the charm of Gilic Ruagh (Gilic the Red), which are proof against cannon fire. He was full of these superstitions, for Christian doctrine had made only a slight impression on the older pagan beliefs of his people. But we did get through the gauntlet of fire to Cambridge. Many of the houses in Cambridge were burning, and the streets were a turmoil of refugees from the battle and others who had taken no part in it. I put the Maclaren down in the doorway of a house, and he thanked me by cursing me for taking him from the battle, saying I had disgraced him by running from the redcoats.

"We dinna run at Drummossie Muir," he said. "There's too much Sassenach in ye."

I was suddenly angry with him, with his fierce pride and his readiness to call others coward and hold them inferior to himself in courage and manliness. I grabbed him by the front of his deerskin jacket and shook him, forgetting his wound, and roared, "Hang you for a miserable, canting, ungrateful dog. I saved your life and you rate at me for doing it."

"Get me spirits," he said, "and leave me alone."

I found a tavern where some casks of rum had been broached by looters, brought a pannikin to him, and left him with it, for I was too angered to stay with him.

The streets of Cambridge, which was no big town, were now in a welter of confusion, though there was no panic. All around, on every hand, the people were arguing about what should be done now. Some were erecting barricades, others were trying to load wagons to leave the place. The men of the militia companies had lost their officers, and there was no one to command them. They were in a bad mood, feeling that, if they had been reinforced or if more ammunition had been sent to them, they could have held the trench against the British.

It was the general opinion that the battle had been lost only through lack of ammunition, and I believe to this day that this was true. But those who had remained behind the lines in Cambridge said that it had been impossible to get more men or more powder to the trenches, as the neck of land connecting the peninsula with the mainland had been so heavily bombarded during the action that no one could get across it alive.

I found my father in the streets of Cambridge. He was standing on a table outside a tavern, trying to restore some order in the mob around. He wanted those who had arms and powder to get out of the town and form some kind of defense line out of range of the guns of the British ships.

Several saw the sense of his suggestion, and finally some kind of order was restored, as captains and other officers rounded up groups of their men and led them off. Some were put to defense and others to getting food and others to guarding food shops and taverns, so that by late evening matters in Cambridge were under control. I helped with this work, and when it was done had a few moments alone with my father.

"What do you think is to happen now?" I asked.

"A siege," he replied. "The British have gained nothing. They have won a small strip of land across the river from Boston, but if matters are properly managed, we can put entrenchments on the mainland all around the city and cut them off from their food supplies. If we keep at it long enough, we can starve them out and force them to evacuate."

It was a mark of the coolness of my father that, while I had in mind only the battle which we had fought and lost, he had taken a sweeping view not of the battle but of the military situation, and found that the advantage still lay with us.

"Surely," I said, "there is sufficient food in Boston to last the British for a great many months."

"No," said my father. "I know the city well and know its food supplies well. It is midsummer. No harvest supplies have reached Boston, which has to live off food from the mainland. The flour in the city is what is left over from last year's harvest. Supplies of salt beef will be low, awaiting the butchering of animals which, as you should know, is only done later in the year to save feeding them through the winter. The city has no supplies of firewood. And furthermore it has a large population to support. Mark my words, if we besiege them now, they will be hungry in a month and starving in four."

"And what if they attack?" I asked.

"We gave them such a drubbing on the hill there that I doubt they will try it until reinforced. It will take a month for the news of this battle to get to England, another month for the Ministry to decide to reinforce the garrison in Boston, and another two months to get the troops over. Personally I do not think they will be reinforced."

"You make things seem very hopeful for us," I said.

"Perhaps I am too optimistic," replied my father. "We have several serious handicaps, any one of which may be critical. The enlistment of the men in the militia companies is due to expire. After the battle the men may decide to go home to their farms. After all, they have the harvest to get in. If they go they will take their guns with them, for their guns are their own possessions. In a few weeks we may have no army here at all.

"Again we have no gunpowder and no sources of gunpowder in the colonies. All our powder has been imported—largely from the West Indies. We must continue to get powder from the West Indies or wherever else we can. That means bringing it in ships, with the British Navy determined to prevent such ships reaching our ports.

"Finally we have no real leader. What has happened so far is that the New England colonies have taken up arms against the Crown in protection of their rights. But will the other colonies support them? Will they join the fight, or will they decide to be discreet and stay out, hoping that, even at this late date, matters can be patched up with England?"

"Do you think they will be patched up?" I asked.

"No," said my father. "After Concord and Lexington and now this, matters have gone too far. The issue must be decided now by force of arms—the colonies against England." He spoke these words sadly, and I knew that the rebellion grieved him, for he had always been loyal to King George III.

"What if we win?" I asked. "What then?"

"Then there will be a new nation brought into being —the American nation."

"And if we lose?"

"Perhaps they will hang us side by side, son," said my father almost wistfully.

3

Within twenty-four hours of the battle which became
known as the Battle of Bunker Hill, though it was
fought on Breed's Hill to the south of Bunker Hill, there
was no sign of confusion or indecision in our lines.

They were a feverish twenty-four hours, for, a coun-
cil of war having been summoned by General Artemus
Ward (who at the time was in charge of the colonial
troops), it was agreed that we must encircle Boston
with trenchworks and redoubts and gun positions so as
to put the city in a state of seige.

The decision was no sooner taken than the orders were given and the men set to work. All who were able took a hand in the digging of the entrenchments. Even the women in Cambridge came out to do what they might—some supplying food and water, others actually working with mattock and shovel. I saw General Ward myself—and he was an elderly man—working away in one section of the trenches with a pick.

The only man who willingly withheld himself from the task was, I believe, the Maclaren of Spey. True, with his wounded arm, he had sufficient excuse. But it was not his wound that prevented the Maclaren bearing a hand so much as his pride. He said plainly and loudly that this kind of work was not suited to the chieftain of a clan. It was not a fighting man's work but the occupation of menial men, and he would not take any part in it. He had dressed his wound himself, out of a medicine bag he carried which contained powdered herbs and flakes of bark, whose uses he had learned from the Indians in Carolina. I had by now got over some part of my anger at him and asked him how he felt.

He did not even look up as I approached, but stared angrily at the ground in front of him. I knew these moods well. They might last a day or they might last a month. But when his disposition was such as at present, the Maclaren of Spey was best left alone.

So I went off to help with the entrenchment, and this angered him even more. He came up to me after a while and asked why I disgraced him by doing the work of farmers. Since almost all the men around were farmers, this remark did not sit well with them.

"Have you aught against farmers?" asked the Medford man who had been in the trenches with us.

"I have," said the Maclaren, his eyes glittering with the black mood that was on him. "There is no a gentleman among five thousand o' them."

"By thunder," said the man, "if you were not wounded, I'd flatten you with this spade, little man."

That was just what the Maclaren needed. "Gie yon dirt digger yir hunting knife, Peter," he said to me.

"No," I cried. "Leave the man alone."

"Gie him yir knife," thundered the Maclaren.

"I'm as good a man as you are," said the Medford farmer doggedly. I could see that he was nervous, and yet he did not want to back down.

"We'll see," said the Maclaren. Since I would not part with my own knife, he took his and threw it on the ground between them.

"Now," said the Maclaren, white with rage, "pick up the *sgean dhu* (black knife), and I'll hae it from ye in a minute and slit you like a herring."

The farmer hesitated. There was no doubt but that the Maclaren meant what he said. He looked around at the others, some of whose faces were grave, some angry, and some grinning.

"Any one of ye pick it up," said the Maclaren, "if he thinks he's a better man than me."

But none of them would do it, and he took the knife himself and walked off from them without as much as a glance backward. It had been a childish and bullying gesture on his part, but when he was angry he did such things.

It was the custom in those early days for the men to elect their own officers. Late that night the men of the Maclaren's company, of whom the Medford man was one, called a meeting with the object of ousting the Maclaren and electing in his stead one of their own kind. I was at the meeting, being myself a member of the company, and I said plainly that I did not blame the men but that they should understand that the Maclaren was a man of moods. He would stand by them to the last if they were in trouble, but he would not allow himself to be crossed or slighted in the smallest degree, such was the fierceness of his pride.

"We don't want a man like that over us," said one. "He's not our sort and is as savage as an Indian. We're peaceful men and decent men, respectful of each other's rights, and won't be bullied and browbeaten by a half-savage from Carolina."

"He ought to go back to the frontier," said another. "We don't need his sort in New England."

So the talk went, and several candidates were proposed as a substitute for the Maclaren. But, curiously, when the votes were taken, none had a clear majority, and many of the men voted for the Maclaren despite his foul temper and proud bearing because of the way he had picked off the British during the battle with his rifle. In the end he stayed as their captain, though I cannot pretend that he had at the time the loyalty of his whole company. Many indeed spoke of leaving and joining some other militia group.

Two days later, however, an incident occurred which altered the men's thinking on the subject of the Scotsman. One of our company, having slipped into Cambridge without leave and drunk more than he could hold, was brought back by the provost guard and handed over to the Maclaren for punishment.

The charge was a serious one—absent without leave while on active service and drunkenness—and it carried an automatic penalty of flogging.

But the Maclaren angrily refused to flog the man.

"What punishment do you propose?" the colonel asked.

" 'Tis my business," said the Maclaren and would say nothing further.

The punishment consisted of having the offender parade for a week with an empty rum bottle in his hand instead of his musket, which was taken from him for that period. The public shame weighed deeply on the man, and he never offended again.

The discovery that the man was not to be flogged, as he could have been by another captain, warmed the rest of the company to the Maclaren, and talk of replacing him died away. In time the men became proud of their savage captain, and they talked of themselves with pride as "Maclaren's men."

The Maclaren proved his worth to them in many other ways too. When the entrenchments had been dug, each company faced the task of building shelters, for we were to camp in the field. The Maclaren's men were the best housed of all, for he showed them not only how to build rainproof and windproof shelters, but how to ventilate them so that when we had to cook indoors because of rain, we were not smoked out. He had them cut drains around each hut so that the ground inside was soon hard and dry. And, when it came to food, he saw to it that we were well supplied and the food decently cooked.

These were small things. But the captains of other companies had no experience in such matters, and their men were used to their wives doing their cooking and did not know how to make a good pan bread with flour and sour milk and a little baking soda and so on. They wasted much of their flour supply in concoctions that proved uneatable.

Gradually the men came to believe that the Maclaren was indeed a superior kind of person. But he did not unbend with them. He had no use for what he called "leveling talk" and "cant," which were the terms he applied to any suggestion that men were equal. No man was his equal in his opinion. He was superior and apart from them all, dined alone, insisted on having two soldiers as his personal servants, and would take his wine (for we got some in Cambridge) alone or only with some other officer whom he considered gentleman enough to sit with him.

Soon he was known to all the men in the lines, and, though they might joke about him behind his back, yet they were very careful to be respectful in his presence.

I shared in this respect, for it was common knowledge that the Maclaren had brought me up. I slept in the same hut with him and ate at his table. And when any favor was wanted, it was to me that the men made their application.

Meanwhile we got a new general from Philadelphia —a big man, red-faced, with a nose like a hatchet. He was a man whose name I knew well, for he had campaigned with my father in the French and Indian Wars. He was George Washington, now General Washington. One of his first actions after taking over command from General Ward was to confer with my father, and the upshot of this meeting was that my father was sent to Philadelphia on some special mission of which he would give me but meager details.

"I can say nothing except that it has to do with the supply of arms," said my father on parting with me.

"Gunpowder?" I queried.

He nodded. "Gunpowder," he said. "Every pound of gunpowder is precious. A pound today is worth a ton a year from now. Without it we will fail, and if we fail life will not be worth living."

He turned then to the subject of the Maclaren of Spey and my relationship with him. "I know you love him," he said, "and owe him loyalty. But he is a dangerous man."

"In what way dangerous?" I asked.

"In his ideas," said my father gravely. "His heart is not in this cause. He fights to avenge his clan. He thinks of you as a member of his clan and will demand obedience from you that must conflict with your duty to these colonies."

"I can handle him," I said.

"I trust you can," replied my father. "But the task is greater and more complicated than any boy of your age should have to undertake. You would not come to Philadelphia with me? I could find you employment there and get you out of these difficulties."

"No," I said. "I will not leave the Maclaren."

"That is what I feared," said my father heavily, and with that we parted.

The Maclaren was glad to see my father go. That was because he loved me so much, and, with his own sons dead and all his kin, needed me to take their place. He had indeed, during our days in the wilderness, bound me to him as a natural son by making a cut in his wrist and mine and mingling the blood together. This, he said, made us of one blood so that my enemies were his enemies and his enemies mine, and we were, in a sense, one and the same person.

So for a while he was more cheerful with me, but as the days dragged into weeks and the weeks into months and there was nothing to relieve the tedium of the siege, he became morose again and talked of leaving and going back to Carolina.

The first few times he mentioned this project I paid little heed, feeling that he was just working off a black mood. But when he became more insistent and even set a day for our leaving (for he was quite sure that I would go with him), I said that we were members of the Continental Army, fighting for the cause of the colonies, and could not leave whenever we pleased.

At this he flew into a towering rage. He did not give a fig for the colonies, he said, nor for any country in the world. He had joined the Continentals because the British had destroyed his clan thirty years before and he must avenge his dead kinsmen.

His concentration on clan loyalty angered me, and I turned on him. "Do you think," I cried, "that the whole world revolves around Drummossie Muir and the extermination of the Maclarens? Do you think that there is no other cause in the world to be fought for? That nothing else matters but that three hundred of the Maclarens were killed by the redcoats thirty years ago?"

"Aye," he said. "Nothing else matters and nothing else should matter to you, for you are a Maclaren, bound to me."

It was on the tip of my tongue to say that I had no interest in his personal vengeance, but fought only for the liberty of the colonies. But something warned me to withhold this declaration. I contented myself by saying that we could not, with honor, leave the cause in which we had voluntarily enlisted.

The mention of honor touched him, and he put aside for a while talk of desertion. Then one day, when we were alone together in the hut, he said to me, "Do ye fancy a little fighting, Peter?"

"What are you planning?" I asked.

"A wee raid on the British at Roxbury," said the Maclaren. "I have no mentioned it to the colonel, he being a soft mon. But taenight I'm taking four men tae the Roxbury lines tae get a prisoner or twa. I'm thinking ye'd like tae come."

"I would," I said. "But you'd better speak to the colonel."

"There's nae need," said the Maclaren. "'Tis a company matter and I hae given meself twenty-four hours' leave for urgent personal business." He paused and then went on. "'Twill be a dark night," he concluded. "Good for hunting."

4

We were lying, myself, the Maclaren, and three men from our company, on the crest of a little knoll, watching the British pickets at their post on Boston Neck outside the city.

We had lain in the darkness in this position for some twenty minutes, studying the pickets and counting those at this particular post. The pickets had a small fire burning. When they threw a new piece of wood on this, the flames leaped up and it was possible to see their faces, which seemed for the moment to be suspended in the air as if they belonged to bodiless heads. We had counted ten men around the fire, but suspected that there were others in the darkness. Still we reasoned there would not be many, for it was a chilly night and there was a keen wind blowing off the waters of the bay. Those then who were not asleep would likely be gathered around the fire.

The Maclaren, lying upon his belly and peering through the withered tufts of grass on the top of the little knoll, now gave his orders.

"I'm going tae circle tae the right wi' Peter," he said. "The three of ye stay here until ye've counted tae a hundred. Then fire. Dinna all fire taegither but one at a time. Gie them three roonds apiece and then get back tae the lines. Ye remember the password?"

"Plowshares," said one of the men.

"And the countersign?"

"Plow horses."

"Guid," said the Maclaren. "Dinna wait fer the laddie and me. We'll be back wi' a prisoner." He handed his musket to one of the men and I did the same, for in the work ahead we had no need of guns, and then we moved off to the right. We did not crawl but ran swiftly, doubled up and zigzagging, our moccasined feet making no noise on the grass that could be heard above the wind.

When we had gone a hundred paces the Maclaren stopped and unloosed from around his waist a long length of rope. He had tied to one end of this a small skin pouch in which there were some thirty bullets. He now turned to me.

"Flush me a turkey," he said.

I knew the tactic well, for I had used it before in attacks on the Indian settlements in the Carolinas. I drew my hunting knife and cut a sod out of the grass with it. It was a big sod, and I flung it in the direction of the British outpost. At the same time there was the explosion of a musket to our rear and left as the three men we had left on the knoll opened fire on the pickets.

From immediately in front of the Maclaren where the turf had fallen a voice called, "Who goes there?" and this was immediately followed by the discharge of a musket. The Maclaren hurled the weighted end of the line around his head and then let it go in the direction from which the musket had been fired. He immediately hauled in on the line, which jerked tight. There was a cry of "help" from the darkness, and I leaped on the British sentry, who was entangled with the line, jerked him to his feet, and put my hunting knife in his back.

"Move," I ordered, and thrust him in the direction of the Maclaren.

But the sentry was a bolder man than I had reckoned on. He let out another bawl for help, and two other figures appeared out of the darkness, visible even in the gloom by their white breeches and crossed bandoliers. This was more resistance than we had bargained for.

I whirled around and struck one of the newcomers with a clenched fist in the belly. The man went to his knees, and I yelled to the Maclaren to run while he could. Then I grappled with another of the soldiers and bore him to the ground, but someone else leaped on me and I was cuffed and buffeted, and finally, my arms pinned behind me, dragged to my feet to find a soldier facing me with his bayonet at my chest.

"Murderous dog," said the soldier, white with fury, "I should kill you now."

"They got the sergeant," cried another. "Tomahawked. Kill 'im and 'ave done with it. They're Indians."

The point of the bayonet was pressed so hard against my chest that it pierced my deerskin tunic, and I could feel a little trickle of blood on my skin. I expected that the bayonet would be driven home, and it might well have been if three men had not come out of the darkness dragging with them the Maclaren of Spey who still kicked and struggled.

He was brought to me and since he still fought against his captors one of the soldiers pulled out a pistol and clubbed him with it and the Maclaren went limp.

"We'd better take them back to the captain," one soldier said, "for questioning."

"Fat lot of good it will do to question them," said another. "They're Mohawks. They won't say nothing."

"That's for the captain to decide," said the first man. "I'm in charge here now. Come on, march 'em off." And so we were taken through the British lines, the Maclaren being dragged along by two men who held him under the arms. We were conducted to a small hut about two hundred yards behind the picket and left there under guard. My arms were tied behind me and my legs were tied also. The Maclaren was also trussed, though he was unconscious. After a while the Maclaren regained his senses and looked around him warily. He saw me but said nothing, for he was not a man given to unnecessary talk.

"You'll 'ang," one of the guards said to the Maclaren, seeing he had regained his senses. "Won't take long," he added. "About twenty minutes for the big 'un"—nodding toward me— "You might take 'arf an 'our though, being lighter, see."

For reply the Maclaren spat at him, being rewarded by a cuff.

After a little while we were taken from the hut to the quarters of a captain of infantry. He was a thin, fair-haired man in his early twenties. He wore his hair long and pulled back severely into a pigtail at the back of his head.

He was playing a game of cards with another officer when we were brought in, and neither of the officers deigned to look up as we entered the room. Instead they continued with the game, leaving us standing just inside the doorway with guards on either side and behind us.

Only when they were through with the hand did the young, fair-haired officer look at us, leaning back in his chair and raising an eyebrow as if he were surprised by our presence.

"Ah," he said. "Prisoners, I see. Where were they taken, corporal?"

"At the picket on the Boston Neck, sir," said the corporal and gave the story. He made a great deal of the fact that we had been armed with tomahawks and knives, which he plainly regarded as barbarous and unfair weapons, and our using them a circumstance which must, of itself, lead to execution.

"Well, what have they to say for themselves?" said the captain, picking up the deck of cards and shuffling them, as if he really did not much care what we had to say for ourselves, though he was obliged to put the question.

"Begging your pardon," said the corporal, "I think they are Indians and don't understand. Leastways they ain't said nothing so far and don't look like civilized people."

"Corporal," said the captain, continuing with his shuffling, "you have eyes?"

"Yes, sir."

"What color are they, pray?"

"Blue, sir."

"And what color are the prisoners' eyes?"

The corporal looked at mine. "Blue, sir," he reported.

"Ah," said the captain. "And have you now discovered in these parts a race of blue-eyed Indians?"

To this the corporal made no reply, and the captain stood up and walked over to me, and standing but a foot from me looked keenly into my face and then fingered the deerskins in which I was clad. He did the same with the Maclaren and then returned to the table and sat down.

"Not Indians, corporal," he said. "Frontiersmen. Pennsylvania, perhaps, or farther south. The Carolinas maybe. Worse than Indians in fact because they don't fight for pay. They fight because . . . er . . . they wish to fight. Having lived without the benefit of law for most of their lives, they rather naturally resent law.

"You," he said, turning suddenly to me. "What is your name, fellow?"

I cannot say that I had any fear of the man. Rather his attitude angered me, and I said, "Peter Treegate, and yours?" He smiled but did not reply to this, and the guard beside me struck me a blow on the cheek to teach me, I suppose, to be more respectful to this captain.

"Hmmmmm . . ." said the officer, "an English name. In fact, a Boston name. There was a certain merchant of this town loyal to the King to the very eve of the present hostilities. John Treegate. Any relation?"

"He is my father."

"Ah," said the officer. "Now I recall. You are the son who disappeared and was brought up in the wilds during your father's absence on a mission in England. The story created quite a stir around town. And you?" turning to the Maclaren.

"I am the Maclaren of Spey."

"An outlaw, no doubt," said the captain.

"A chieftain," said the Maclaren, "and the enemy of yir fat German Georgie in London."

I believe that the guard would have struck him as I

had been struck, but he saw such a look both of hatred and scorn on the Maclaren's face that he was quelled by it, and merely pulled at the ropes that bound him.

The captain was not shaken by the answer. He coolly took a piece of paper and a quill and wrote a few lines on it, the scratching and squeaking of the pen being the only noise in the small room. When he had done this he dusted the paper with sand, blew the sand off, wiped off those particles which had fallen upon his white breeches, and read what he had written.

Colonel Sir John Moresby Pett KC
Commanding 14th Light Infantry,
Boston

I have the honor to inform you that my pickets have taken two of the rebels who made an attack upon our lines in which Sergeant Thomas Fielding was tomahawked and killed. The rebels have identified themselves as Peter Treegate, son of John Treegate, late of the city of Boston, and one who styles himself the Maclaren of Spey.

I have examined the two of them and listened to the evidence of witnesses, etc., etc., and submit for your approval that they should be hanged for murder.

Awaiting your word on this judgment, I have the honor to remain, sir,

Your obedient Servant,
John Richfield, Captain

Post Scriptum. I have reason to suspect that the one calling himself the Maclaren of Spey may well be an outlaw from Scotland following the Jacobite rising. In this case his being hung at the present time would merely complete a sentence deferred these many years.

When he had read this to us in a voice as casual as if he were but passing the time of day, the captain asked whether we had any comment to make upon it.

I was amazed at the coolness wherewith he recommended that we be hung, and angered too.

"Murder?" I cried. "We are not murderers but soldiers, as you are. We are not to be taken out and hung without trial or consideration. You are not judge, jury, and hangman over me."

"Soldiers?" said the young captain with a sneer. "And in whose army, pray? I will tell you what you are. You are a rebel, damn you. And you have murdered a sergeant of my company wearing the King's uniform. And you will hang for it, and that very shortly and there is an end to it."

And with that he nodded to the guards, and we were, with no more ceremony, taken from his presence to the small hut in which we had first been lodged. But it was not long before we were escorted from there a distance of perhaps half a mile to a large house on the outskirts of Boston.

I thought we were being taken to be hung and my mouth was dry with fear, and I kept assuring myself that it was impossible that we were to be executed in such an out-of-hand fashion. But I knew that in war such things had happened before and could get no comfort from my own assurances.

The house to which we were taken was heavily guarded by sentries, and we were handed over to four of these and, to my intense relief, conducted into a room of the house; reached by its own door which opened directly on the garden around.

The room into which we were taken had served in happier times as the library of some gentleman. The walls were lined with bookshelves, the books being handsomely bound in leather. There was a large table at one end of the room, a very handsome piece of furniture indeed, and behind this table was sitting a short blocky man in the uniform of a colonel of the British Infantry.

He looked indeed in the moment that we saw him like a portrait in oils. The light from a lamp struck across the scarlet shoulders of his uniform, illuminating the top of his white wig. His hands were held before him on the desk, and he was holding a single piece of paper. His face was hidden from us in shadows, and he did not look up as we entered, but, still studying the paper before him, he said, "You may leave them with me, guard. Remain outside the door but within call."

"Yes, sir," said the corporal who was in charge of the guards, and withdrew with them. And so we stood there, bound, watching the blocky man who was studying the piece of paper which contained a recommendation that we be hung. We were several minutes in this position, myself in a sweat of anxiety, before Sir John Pett casually put down the paper on the table before him and looked up at us. I was aware immediately of a long nose, not fat but prominent and quite out of proportion to the rest of his features, dark eyes, deep-set in his face, and broad black eyebrows which produced a striking effect under his white wig. His face was stern but not cruel, and I drew a crumb of comfort from this.

Sir John looked casually at the two of us, first at the Maclaren, then at me, and then back again at the Maclaren. Something about the Maclaren seemed to strike him, for he stared at him, and then, arising, picked up the oil lamp upon his desk and came swiftly over to the Scotsman.

He held the lamp close to him and examined his features minutely. The light from the lamp illuminated the stone in the tara brooch which the Maclaren had pinned to his tunic, and, from studying the features of the highlander, Sir John turned to the brooch and the stone. This plainly interested him greatly, for he reached out and touched it with his fingers, almost as if to assure himself that it was there. Then he returned to his desk and sat for some moments in silence.

"You are the Maclaren of Spey?" he said at length, addressing the highlander.

"I am," said the other, drawing himself more erect despite his bonds.

"We have met before, you and I," said Sir John. "Thirty years ago when we were much younger men. At Culloden, which you call Drummossie Muir."

The Scotsman said nothing.

"It was you who brought me down with your claymore," said Sir John. "You were in the forefront of the Highland charge. I will never forget your face."

"The Maclarens were given the honor of leading the charge," said the highlander. "Even before the Stuarts of Appin and the MacDonalds of the Isles."

"That brooch of yours," said Sir John, and it seemed to me that he was now making an effort to keep his voice casual, "none have such a brooch but the chieftain of the clan?"

"None."

"I fancy I have seen one like it."

"Where?" demanded the highlander.

Sir John shrugged. "I forget," he said. "I may be mistaken. In any case, these symbols of authority among you highlanders all look alike." He picked up the sheet of paper which he had put on the desk and looked it over.

"It is recommended, and upon good grounds, that you should both be hung," he said. "If I did my duty that is precisely what I should order. Yet hanging is a miserable end for a soldier, and"—with a wry smile—"I know you to be a soldier."

The Maclaren laughed. It was an unexpected laugh —hard and bitter and it shocked me. "Ye hanged the wounded after Drummossie Muir," he said. "Wi' the women and children watching. And then ye hanged the women and children."

"Silence," thundered Sir John, his face purple with

rage. "Silence, I say." He got up from his chair in such a passion that he knocked it over and strode from behind his desk to stand directly before the Maclaren. "I took no part in those hangings," he stormed. "It was no work of mine."

The Maclaren stared at him coldly, his eyes full of hate.

"Do you hear what I say?" stormed Sir John. "I took no part in those hangings. There is no taint or stain of them on me."

Still the Maclaren said nothing, and Sir John turned from him quickly and strode to a window of the room where he stood, his hands clasped behind him, staring out into the cold and darkness of the garden. Frightened as I was, and I admit to fear, for I could still fancy the noose being put around my neck, it occurred to me for a moment that what Sir John was staring at through the window was not the wretched neglected garden of the house, but back through three decades to the time of a terrible battle in the Scottish Highlands and an even more terrible slaughter which had followed it. He was some minutes getting control of himself and then he turned and addressed me from where he was standing by the window.

"How old are you?" he said, and his tone was no longer angry.

"I will be seventeen in a month," I replied.

"This man here," nodding to the Maclaren, "he is a friend of yours—a relative? Or are you merely comrades?"

"He is my foster father," I replied.

"Your foster father?" echoed Sir John.

"Yes."

He considered this information for a while, and then went to the desk, picked up the sheet of paper which contained the recommendation that we should be hung, read it through, and, crumpling it into a ball, threw it into the fireplace.

He then rang a bell on his desk and the corporal appeared with the guard.

"Take these two away," said Sir John. "They are to be interned as prisoners of war. The recommendation for their hanging is disallowed."

I do not believe that I have ever heard more welcome words in all my life.

5

We were taken first to the common jail in the city of Boston, where we were lodged for two weeks, and then to a barge in the harbor which had been converted into a floating jail for the detention of prisoners of war. The common jail had been bad enough, for it was crowded, not only with war prisoners but with prisoners of the civil authorities, with pickpockets and forgers and murderers. The cells were small and so many jammed into them that only half the occupants could find the space to sit on the floor at any one time.

But, bad as the common jail had been, it was as nothing compared to the floating barge into which we were transferred. The barge was completely decked over, and there was not room below the decks for a man to stand upright. When the hatches were opened to put us below, such a stench arose that I was nauseated. But we were thrust into the hold, which was jammed with prisoners so that we had to fight for room for ourselves.

Ventilation, we found, was provided only by a few portholes, and the men fought to get to these to be relieved of the foul air.

We stayed in this floating jail for many weeks. The death rate was high, the dead being taken away in whaleboats at the end of each day. But one meal a day —of a soup made sometimes of corn and sometimes of potato peeling and fish—was served. And, but for the spirit of the Maclaren, I believed many times that in the miserable weeks that followed I would go out of my mind.

The Maclaren was not to be broken, however. A desperate man, he seemed to feed upon desperation. He told his jailers many a time that when he had a chance he would kill them, and was unmercifully flogged twice for flinging his miserable bowl of soup in the face of the man who brought it to him. I begged him not to make trouble for himself, but to no avail. He was a man who could not compromise. Even after his first flogging (which all were compelled to witness), when he regained consciousness, his first words were to curse the "damned Sassenach bloody backs." In the end his savage defiance worked to his benefit, and many of our guards began to fear him, and even attempted to come to terms with him, showing him an occasional favor in the hopes of placating him. The favors were small, but in so miserable a place a morsel of tobacco or any extra piece of bread, as hard as a stone and green with mold, could lighten half a day for us.

Each day after dark, we were taken up on deck for a short period of exercise. In order to move about at all, we had to carry in our hands the twenty-pound shot to which we were chained. Many of the men were too weak to do this, and so had to stand shivering on the deck (for it was now midwinter) during the exercise period. Others, weaker still, were unable to get up to the deck at all, and these invariably died within a day or two. It was pitiful to see the poor wretches making the attempt to get on the deck as if they were climbing out of their graves, and indeed the feat had that significance for them, for, as I have said, those too weak to gain the deck during the exercise period soon died. For myself I still retained a measure of my strength, and shuffled around with the shot in my hands, determined by this exercise to keep up my strength as much as I could as a means of preserving my life.

One day, when we had been two months aboard this floating prison, we were paraded on deck before dark and an officer read to us a proclamation stating that anyone who wished to serve in the forces of His Majesty the King would receive immediate pardon and release and would be enrolled in the army or navy at the regular rate of pay and all his past offenses forgotten.

A whaleboat was brought alongside, and the officer who read this application, looking at the miserable, shackled prisoners, said, "Come, lads. Your plight will not be any worse than it is at present. A good dinner of roast beef will put new strength in you, and your chains will be struck off as soon as you are ashore in Boston."

Two or three of the men shuffled forward and were joined by a dozen others. The officers looked them over and frowned, for they were for the most part older men. He turned to me, for I was taller than the rest of the prisoners and younger too.

"You're a likely young lad," he said. "Why don't you clear yourself with your king and strike a blow like a true man for your country?"

"I have no king," I said bitterly, "and will serve none."

"You're a fool, lad," said the officer, not unkindly. "I'd sooner have a dozen of you than a score of the Germans who will soon be crowding into these colonies."

"Germans?" I said.

"Aye," said the officer. "We are to be reinforced by Hessians, Waldeckers, Brunswickers, and Hanovarians. Then we will thrust out of Boston and put an end to this nonsense in a week. You'd better clear yourself while you have the chance."

But I shook my head. "Your case must be hard," I

said, "when you have to hire German mercenaries to finish the work you started at Breed's Hill."

The officer flushed but said nothing.

Since no more offered their services in return for freedom, the volunteers were loaded into the whaleboat to the jeers and taunts of those who had decided to remain. It was a cold and bitter evening, with a wind from the northeast flecking the pale gray waters of the bay with a dirty white foam. The men were clumsy getting down the short ladder from the barge into the whaleboat, for they were still shackled and had to carry the twenty-pound shot in one hand, using the other to hold onto the ladder. One of them missed his footing and fell into the water between the whaleboat and the barge. I was standing near the edge of the barge and saw this. The man was a short fellow and the water came up to his shoulders. He was hauled out sobbing with terror.

When we had been taken below again, I whispered to the Maclaren, "Did you see the man that fell overboard?"

"Aye," said the Maclaren.

"He was a man of about your size," I said.

"He would have made a lap dog for a mouse," bristled the Maclaren.

"Listen," I said, "he was about the same size as you, and the water only came up to his shoulders."

"What of it?" asked the Maclaren.

"This," I said. "The tide was on the ebb with two

more hours to go. Do you know what that means? If we could get overboard, we could wade ashore."

The Maclaren said nothing for a while, thinking the matter over. Then he said, "They'd shoot us in the water."

"I've thought about that," I said. "Have you ever noticed how this barge is moored?"

"I have not," said Maclaren in such a tone as to indicate that such matters, being connected with the sea, were below his dignity, for he was a man of the land.

"Well," I said, "she's made fast with but one cable, so she swings with the tide. That cable is aft, and is tied to a wooden pin in a rail. I've often watched it."

"So?" said the highlander.

"If I pulled the pin out," I said, "the barge would drift down the bay with the ebb tide."

"And we with it," said the Maclaren.

"No," said I. "We'd be overboard and soon out of musket range, and it would be dark. Are you willing to try? This evening when we're let out for air?"

The Maclaren thought for a minute. "I am," he said eventually.

"Good," I said. "I'll attend to the pin. When I pull it out jump over the stern. I'll follow you. And keep under water for as long as you can hold your breath, until the barge has had a chance to drift away."

I told the other men what was planned, risking a chance that there might be an informer among them. I reasoned that the more who made the venture the better chance we would have of escaping.

Some were excited at the prospects of escape. But more were dubious and advised against making the attempt, saying I would either be shot or drowned in the water. One, who had been a fisherman before he joined a Maine company for the fight at Bunker Hill where he had been captured, advised me especially against the attempt.

"The British aren't fools," he said. "They know that a man can stand in the water around the barge at low tide. But they know too that from here to the shore there are many deep channels and holes—some of them two fathoms even at low tide. And if you step into one of them with that twenty-pound shot and those chains, you will be drowned in a minute."

"Nevertheless, I intend to try," I said. "I'd sooner drown than rot here. What's your name?" I continued. "I haven't seen you before."

"Peace of God Manly," said the man. "One of John Wesley's poor sinners, may the Lord preserve him to everlasting glory, amen."

"I'm Peter Treegate," I said. "When did they bring you here?"

"This morning," said the fisherman.

"Will you make the attempt?" I asked.

"I must consult first with my Maker," said Peace of God. He closed his eyes and then said, loud enough for me to hear, "Beloved Redeemer, who knows the sinfulness and wicked thoughts of all men, here be I a notorious sinner from Salem who, you know, did rob many lobster pots in my wicked days and likewise robbed also the night lines of my poor friends and neighbors, especially George Silvers. And for these sins you have, in your loving-kindness, cast me into this pit of chains that I may sin no more and so gain eternal life through miseries on earth.

"Now I don't want to controvert your ways, in earthly pride and foolishness, Lord, but I be mortal worried about my child Nancy that I have not seen these six long months, that being what you have willed for me. Now here's a chance to get out of this loathsome pit, and I be all shook, not knowing whether it is a wile of Satan to lead me back to my former sinful ways, or whether, in your loving-kindness, Lord, you have relented and say to me as you did to the Leper, 'Depart and sin no more,' so that I may see my Nancy. So do you, Lord, tell me what it is I should do."

This astonishing outburst made me think for the moment that the man was mad. For in the weeks I had been aboard the barge many had taken leave of their senses and spoke of visions and the near approach of Judgment Day. Peace of God remained in silence for a little while, nodding his head at times and then shaking it as if he were being put to the closest examination by the Lord, so that I concluded that he was indeed insane. Then he turned to me and said, "I'll come with you."

I was sorry I had broached that matter to him and got up to leave, but he caught me by the arm. "Now," he said, suddenly very earnest, "I know this bay well.

There's a channel over to the right of this barge that leads to the Roxbury neck, and it's deep even at full ebb. But over to the left, it gets shoal though there's still some holes. If you follow me, trusting in God, without whom nothing can succeed, for we be all sinners and can do nothing for ourselves, we may make it to shore." "Good," I said, and, anxious to be rid of him, went back to the Maclaren.

When we were allowed up on deck after sunset, the wind was blowing even stronger and brought with it a trace of snow. The harshness of the weather served our purpose, for the sentries stayed in the lee of the cabin in which they were quartered to get out of the wind, leaving us to shuffle around the miserable deck for our airing. I, the Maclaren, and the fisherman, Peace of God, as soon as the hatch had been removed, shuffled to the stern of the barge. Several others came with us so that there was a huddle of prisoners on the stern. This shielded me from the sentries, but I had some difficulty loosening the wooden pin to which the mooring line of the barge was fastened. And when I did so I made a disastrous discovery. The mooring line was indeed wrapped around the pin, but the end of it, hidden from me until unwound, was attached to an iron ring embedded stoutly in one of the timbers of the barge. It could not be cut, for we had no knife.

It was no time, however, for hesitating. "Over you go," I said to the Maclaren, and the highlander rolled over the stern of the barge with me behind him. Peace of God followed, but none of the other prisoners, seeing that the barge was still attached to its mooring, took the chance.

For a second we thought ourselves safe, for no immediate alarm was raised. Peace of God took the lead, and the waves lashing around our faces, we struggled off in the ice-cold water. When we had gone only a few steps, however, there was a musket shot from the barge and then two more, and I felt the balls whistle past my head. Then there came a hissing sound, and two rockets soared up and burst in the air over us, illuminating the water around.

More rockets followed and more musket shots, so that the water was peppered with the balls and I expected to be hit at any minute. I looked back and saw the barge's whaleboat coming toward us. There were two soldiers standing near the bows with muskets and three men at the oars. A sixth man stood at the gunwale with a lantern, trying to see into the gloom.

"Down," I yelled to the Maclaren, as the boat came nearer. I grabbed him and pulled him under—it was no hard task, for the water was up to the Maclaren's chin—and held him there for as long as I could hold my breath. But when I came up again the boat was almost on top of us, and I was staring right into the musket barrels of the two soldiers.

"There they are," cried the man with the lantern. "Shoot and be damned to them."

I saw the flash in the pan of one of the muskets and jerked my head aside. But the piece misfired, and the other musket, wetted by the snow which was now coming down much faster, also failed to discharge.

"Grab the oars," roared Peace of God, suiting the action to the words. I grabbed the oar nearest me. The man using it made the error of standing up to wrest it from me. I jerked the oar toward me and then thrust it back, and the man toppled into the water.

Peace of God had served another of the rowers in the same manner, and now a minor panic broke out in the rowboat.

The man with lantern dropped it, and it was immediately extinguished. The Maclaren of Spey managed to haul himself over the stern of the whaleboat by the process of first heaving into the boat the twenty-pound shot to which he was chained. Relieved of its weight, he grabbed the man who had had the lantern, pulled him over on his back, and dumped him into the water. One of the soldiers now jumped overboard of his own free will, and I hauled myself into the boat. There were still two men in the boat. One struck at me with a boat hook, catching me on the shoulder, for I was so numb from the cold that I could move only slowly to defend myself. He struck again, and I got up and grappled with him, and we went over the side together. I lost him in the water, and the Maclaren pulled me out, for I was exhausted. When I got aboard again, we were the sole occupants of the whaleboat.

Peace of God took the two oars that remained aboard and started pulling away from the barge.

Now the problem arose of where to land the boat. The

rockets on the barge had been answered by others ashore, so that the whole waterfront of Boston was alerted, and boats would soon be putting out into the bay in pursuit of them.

The obvious thing to do would be to head south and land on the mainland below Dorchester Heights. But even if we got ashore, we would soon be pursued and, with the iron shot to which we were chained, we would be overtaken and captured. In the boat we could make the same speed as our pursuers and had a head start on them.

"We will head for open water," said Peace of God. "Tide and wind are with us, and I do believe the Lord hath sent them to our aid, miserable sinners though we are."

He then headed the boat out toward the ocean.

6

The prison barge lay between us and the open sea. We could see it as a darker bulk against the black water of the bay, and every now and then the whole area would be lighted up as a rocket was sent off as a signal to those ashore that some prisoners had escaped. These rockets clearly showed our own position, and a storm of musket balls were sent at us, several of which burst through the planking of the old whaleboat, so that she was soon water-logged. Luckily none of us were hit.

Peace of God had now taken over control. He made

me sit in the stern, not on a seat but in the bottom of the boat, and made the Maclaren sit forward, also in the bottom. We were, in this position, up to our chests in water, and since we were going slowly out to sea, I assumed that we would shortly be drowned. The boat would sink and we would be carried down by our shackles.

However, I did not repent our escape, having assured myself that a few more weeks in the prison barge and I would have died anyway. I looked around for something with which to bail and found the cocked hat of one of the soldiers floating in the bottom of the boat. This I put to use and, though I believe we shipped as much water as I was able to throw out, still we did not settle any deeper.

The cold was intense. My legs, feet, arms, and hands were soon without any feeling at all. Once or twice I dropped the hat with which I was bailing and, searching for it in the water in the bottom of the whaleboat, could not feel it with my fingers, so numb had they become. I remember being surprised once, when, having caught sight of the hat and grabbed it, I could not feel the material between my fingers, and had to grip it mightily to assure myself that it was there.

In fifteen minutes, with Peace of God rowing steadily, we had drawn out of musket range of the barge. But now we saw a rocket go up from the water behind us, perhaps half a mile off. It was soon followed by another, and I was puzzled, for these two rockets had not come from the direction of the barge nor from the Boston waterfront.

Peace of God rested on his oars for a moment to study them. "Frigate," he said. "They've put out after us."

He started rowing again in short quick strokes, and I turned desperately to my bailing, hoping to lighten the boat so we could make more speed. Then I heard the Maclaren shout, "There's a ship ahead."

We all stared into the darkness out to sea. For a while I could see nothing and then made out a dark shape on the water, and my heart sank, for I was sure that we were caught between two British vessels and would soon be retaken.

"Ship ahoy," piped Peace of God in a shaky voice.

"Isn't she another frigate?" I shouted.

"No," he said. "Trading brig—and off course too."

How he could make this out I do not know. But he started rowing again, and I and the Maclaren shouted, "Ship ahoy," for here indeed was salvation if we could attract the attention of this new vessel. I could see her more readily now, for she was much nearer. She was clawing her way into the harbor and seemed intent on passing us perhaps a quarter of a mile off. I concluded that nobody aboard could hear our cries and shouted all the louder. Then the vessel came up into the wind, no more than a hundred yards from us, and stood there with her canvas cracking with a report like gunfire.

"She's seen us," cried Peace of God and, pulling at his oars, soon had us alongside.

I was the first on deck, hauling myself out of the whaleboat and throwing a line down to Peace of God. The other two followed, and two or three men gathered around us, one of them holding a lantern.

"Who the devil are you?" demanded the man, holding the lantern up to inspect us.

"Sinful children of the world," said Peace of God, "cast out of the deep as was Jonah from the mouth of the whale that they may testify to the mercy of their Maker. This will be the brig *Betsy*, if I'm not mistaken," he added with a measure of cunning.

"It is," said the man with the lantern, whom I took to be an officer.

"Then you'd better haul your wind and get out of here," said Peace of God. "There's a frigate coming down the bay toward you."

"A frigate?" bellowed the officer. "Why, damn your eyes, what do you mean by bringing a frigate down on us?" I do not know what reply was expected to this question, but the officer, whom I later found to be a certain Tom Felton, first mate, did not stop for one. He started roaring orders to slacken braces and haul sheets and set topsails, and in a moment the decks were all confusion with men running here and there to obey his commands. Peace of God, who seemed immediately at home on the brig, led us to a small roundhouse aft of the foremast where we found the cook—who also served as ship's carpenter and smith—and asked him to strike the shackles off us.

He knew the cook, a surly individual who smelled of

rum, and while the cook was busy with our shackles, grumbling mightily, Peace of God lectured him on the evils of slavery to alcohol. I was frozen to the bone and so weary that my head was in a whirl, and yet I could not help smiling at some of the snatches of conversation between Peace of God and the cook which went like this:

Cook: "Hold steady. I cannot strike right if you move about."

Peace of God: "Steady it is, mate, and steady the road that leads to salvation. Nor should a man pause to drink of the foul pools which lie beside this road, for these are but snares of Satan."

Cook: "You look to your own soul, Peace of God, and I'll look to these shackles."

Peace of God: "Ah, friend, the bonds which you strike from me are light as straws compared with those which I seek to strike from thee. For thou art bound around with the coils of intemperance and caught in the net of wantonness and about to be drawn down into the depths of hell for all time. Yet I will try to save thee."

Cook: "Do you think I must go to hell, then?" At the word "hell" he struck so mightily on the shackle that it broke immediately.

Peace of God: "Aye. Unless you mend your ways and first put aside the use of rum and also tea and smoking tobacco."

Cook: "So I will, Peace of God. So I will. When I am older and no longer at sea and do not need them."

The Maclaren meanwhile had been peering around the hole of the cabin in which we were crowded and, spying a pannikin hidden behind some woolens on a tiny shelf, contrived to get it down and swallowed the contents at one gulp.

"Hey," cried the cook. "What do you think you're doing?"

"Helping you tae salvation," said the Maclaren sourly. "Now strike off my irons."

Peace of God looked at him sorrowfully. "You are not a man of God," he said. "You have much to suffer before you can be cleansed and brought to repentance."

"Dinna preach at me, ye canting Whig," snarled the Maclaren. "Here, you. Get these irons off me."

I was all but asleep when my turn came to get the shackles off, and when this was done found my way to the forecastle and, dropping on one of the bunks there, fell instantly into a deep slumber through exhaustion.

7

Some hours later, when it was almost dawn, I was awakened and taken with the Maclaren and Peace of God to the cabin aft to see the captain.

The captain, when we entered, was sitting barefooted on the bunk of his tiny cabin. He had one foot in his lap and was gently caressing a large red bunion on the ball of his great toe. Every now and then he would blow on it, as if the bunion were a coal which needed to be kept glowing. He was a small man, very thin, with a curved nose like a sailor's claspknife. He had a few wisps of white hair on his head, and his appearance was that of a man who had received no nourishment for many years, so that all that was left of him was a frame covered with white, loose flesh.

"You're soldiers, I suppose," he said, when he had cooled the bunion sufficiently to give us his attention.

"Yes, sir," I replied. "We're soldiers in the Continental Army."

"Prisoners, I suppose," said the captain, and blew on his bunion again.

"Yes," I said. "We escaped from a prison barge in the bay."

"Men of no property, I assume," said the captain.

"None," I said.

"No money?"

"None."

"And no influence?"

"None."

"Then, hang you, why didn't you drown?" the captain roared. "Answer me that? Why didn't you drown instead of putting my ship in danger? There's a frigate hauling down on me now. I cannot shake her or lose her, and I'm stuffed with gunpowder and not a penny profit for three months' work if I don't fetch Lynn safe and sound. Perdition take you and the whole Continental Army and every farmer's whelp of a soldier in it."

"Little man," said the Maclaren of Spey, "be careful of what you are saying."

"And who the devil are you?" demanded the captain.

"I'm the Maclaren of Spey," said the Scotsman.

"By all that's wonderful," cried the captain, "you mean I risked my ship for a sniveling runaway Jacobite?"

I grabbed the Maclaren quickly, for otherwise he would have thrown himself on the captain. But the captain was not in the slightest disturbed. He continued blowing on his bunion and slowly picked up a horse pistol which had been lying on the bunk beside him and leveled this at the Maclaren, who saw the force of this argument and quieted down.

"Maybe I'll turn a penny on you yet," said the captain. "There's likely a price on your head. But I must think about it."

He turned now to Peace of God and eyed him closely for some minutes. "It seems I know you," he said. "It seems I know you and I don't like you."

"Why, to be sure you know me," said Peace of God. "Brothers we are—in a manner of speaking. Same town we come from. Salem, that is, in Massachusetts. And same trade we followed in days of peace, namely fishing."

"I have it now," said the captain. "Peace of God Manly."

"Aye," said the other. "And many a lobster I lifted from your pots in my sinful days, George Silvers. Though I've prayed for forgiveness ever since, as I'm praying for you now."

"And why are you praying for me now?" asked the other.

"Because, God forgive you, you are a black-hearted,

double-dealing son of Satan," said Peace of God, as mildly as if he were remarking that it was a fair day and the wind gentle and from the right quarters. "I'm praying for you, George Silvers," he continued, "for you are a willful man and a bold man and a headstrong man, and you have one overbearing lump of wickedness in you that can only be dissolved by prayer."

"And what's that?" said Captain Silver.

"Love of money," said Peace of God. "But remember, George Silvers, that it is of no profit to a man if he gain the whole world but lose his own soul."

"You keep your soul, Peace of God," said Silvers, "and I'll take my profit where I can find it. Well," he continued, "my luck isn't completely out, for you are the best pilot for these waters in the whole of New England. So up on deck with you and stand by the helmsman and bring us in safely to Lynn."

"It's the harbor of heaven I want to bring you safely into, George Silvers," said Peace of God.

"Lynn will serve," replied the captain. "If I can make Lynn before that frigate gets within gunshot, I'll rest contented."

He dismissed us with a jerk of his head, and as we were going out told me to call on the cook and have him bring a bucket of hot salt water back to bathe his bunion in.

The seas were still confused when we made the deck, but the wind was easing and the mate, Felton, had shaken out the reef in the mainsail and shaken out the brig's foresail and jib as well, so that she was moving along briskly. Peace of God reported to the mate and said he had orders to pilot the brig to Lynn. He then asked what the soundings had been and when given them, and the nature of the bottom, he then said, "We should haul her more into the wind, for we are twenty miles offshore and cannot make Lynn if we keep on the present bearing."

"Give your orders to the helmsman," said the mate, and Peace of God went back to the tiller and gave the new course.

The Maclaren found a sheltered spot under the lee gunwale and was soon asleep, for he was a man who could sleep in any weather, but I had now enough rest and stayed awake with Peace of God.

"What chance have we of getting away from the frigate?" I asked, for I could see the King's ship through the murk on the horizon.

"A touch more to windward," said Peace of God to the helmsman. "A good chance and a bad one," he said to me.

"What do you mean by that?" I asked, but to this Peace of God made no reply.

For the next three hours, the brig held her course, but the frigate was gaining on us and by nine in the morning was coming up fast. Four miles was beyond the range of her guns, but she would be within range in an hour. And we were still two hours' sailing from Lynn, according to Peace of God.

All plain sail was set on the brig, and gave her an extra two knots, but the *Cerebus*, for that was the name of the frigate, now broke out her royals, canceling the brig's slight advantage. Ahead was a small rocky island with a welter of white water between it and the mainland. Peace of God eyed the rocky island and then turned to Captain Silver, who had come on the deck upon hearing the report that the frigate was coming down on us fast.

"There's the Barrel of Beef," he said, pointing to the rocky island ahead.

Silvers glanced at the rocky island with the white water between it and the mainland, indicating a submerged reef, and then at the *Cerebus*.

"You've tricked me, you miserable dog!" he cried. "We can't clear the island before the *Cerebus*. We must run out to seaward and she has a start on us and can cut us off."

"We can slip through the Hell Race," said Peace of God. "Tide's on the make, and we will have fourteen feet of water. We draw but twelve and will have two feet between us and the reef."

"You can't take this brig through that gap," stormed Silvers. "There's two miles of reefs and the passage is only a hundred feet wide."

"Straight is the path and narrow the gate to salvation," said Peace of God. "You should reflect on that, George Silvers. There's a power of good in it for you. Get your best helmsman at the tiller, and I will go to the knightheads and give him directions. And have the crew stand by at sheets and braces, for we must use our canvas as well as our rudder."

With that he went forward, being relieved at the helm by another. The Maclaren had now awakened and we went with Peace of God. When the Maclaren saw the expanse of white water which lay ahead of us, an area in which the waves turned swiftly into a creamy foam and jostled and leaped in the air, he announced that they were all going to be drowned and that it was a dog's death for such a man as he.

He knew nothing of the sea and could not swim. He looked longingly at the shore a mile off, and said we ought to take to the boats and get ashore and leave the brig to her fate. A score of dark superstitions concerning the sea, handed down in his clan from generation to generation, rose in his mind—that the last of the Maclarens would be swallowed by a white witch (which he now took to be the angry water before us); that the greatest of the clan (whom he of course took to be himself) would be dragged to his death in the arms of a woman (the brig *Betsy*); and that the bones of the chiefs of the clan would roll unendingly on the bottom of the ocean at the mercy of the tide until Judgment Day.

All these old stories now put him in a mood of deep depression. He had not with him the medicine bag which he normally carried to ward off evil, and he sat on the deck in despair, muttering to himself in Gaelic, and would not be comforted.

"Peace of God will see us safely through the reef," I said in an effort to calm him. But the Maclaren did not think such a thing possible. He was to be drowned. Of that he was convinced, and after a little while he commenced singing a lament for himself, and asked me to remember it, so that if I survived, I could later sing the Lament of the Maclaren, which would comfort him while he searched for his ancestors.

The brig was now almost upon the reef, and I could see a small and twisting channel through it where the water was smoother. This I guessed was the Hell Race. But it was woefully narrow, and the water was sluicing through it as fast as in a quick-flowing river.

"Ease her topsails and jib," shouted Peace of God, and the crew scrambled to carry out his orders.

"Point to larboard and stand by to sheet home," was the next order. On the deck all was now quiet. The men stood by the sheets and braces, their eyes on Peace of God, as if their salvation depended on keeping him closely in sight. The noise of the sea, a hissing noise with below this a deep roar, increased momently.

Waves slapped against the side of the brig and flung upward above the deck in pillars of water, as if the ocean was trying to peep aboard and see how many victims it could claim. The brig went into the Hell Race with the white water writhing on either side, so close that I could have readily thrown a stone into it. The *Betsy's* head fell downwind for a second, and her canvas flogged about with a heavy noise.

"Sheet home," cried Peace of God, and the sails were trimmed and the flapping stopped.

"Steady as you go," cried Peace of God, and the helmsman repeated the order.

The channel ahead was narrowing now, and I saw little beads of perspiration on the end of Peace of God's nose.

"Point to windward," he cried, "and stand by to luff."

The crew were tense at the sheets and braces. They knew that they must trim the sails precisely on the order, and together as one man, for a second's loss could bring disaster.

"Slack the braces," said Peace of God, and the windward braces were eased off.

"Luff all," cried the pilot.

Down went the tiller and the sheets were trimmed in hard. For a second the *Betsy* seemed to stand still in the water. Then she moved sluggishly forward, clawing her clumsy way closer to the wind. I was so fascinated at what was happening that I forgot the danger. Fifty feet ahead I could see an edge of rock with boiling water all around it. The brig headed straight for this, and indeed her long bowsprit was over the white water before she moved blindly to the windward. She skirted the rock by no more then fifteen feet, and above the noise of the water there came a roar of triumph from the crew. But Peace of God showed no sign of relief. The channel here was wider, but it took a sharp turn to seaward a quarter of a mile ahead, and he looked grave.

"Wind's holding back the tide," he said to me. "Up yonder"—pointing to the turn ahead—"is the shallowest part of the Hell Race. If the tide were normal, we would have two feet between us and the bottom. But, as I said, the wind is holding the tide back."

"How much water do you think we will have?" I asked.

"A foot," said Peace of God. "Maybe less."

The brig crept down on the bend, skirting the shoreward side of it. The bend was narrow, and the speed of the water through the Hell Race increased. The current was against us, flowing at four knots through the narrow gap. Peace of God turned for a second and eyed the brig's canvas, but whether he approved of what he saw I could not discover, for he said nothing.

After a little while he called to the helmsman to put his tiller down to leeward, so that we inched closer to the shoreward side of the channel, and I was sure that in a second we would be aground on the reef.

"Stand by to ease the sheets," he called. "We must drive her through, God willing."

We were now at the entrance of the turn, and the Maclaren, sensing the excitement, had got up from the deck and stood staring at the narrow, swiftly flowing channel which lay ahead of us.

"Lee-oh," cried Peace of God. "Let fly the sheets! Drive her through!" The brig swung round to starboard and plunged into the turn. She met the inflowing water on her blunt bows and hesitated, and then, as if summoning all her strength, drove her head against it. She seemed to lift up for a second and then settled down, straining to make her way against the current. Then I heard another noise above that of the surf. I felt rather than heard it. It consisted of a sharp scrape, followed by a rumble and more scraping.

"She's aground!" someone called in a high-pitched voice. The deck bumped heavily beneath my feet. The scraping and rumbling continued, and for a moment the brig seemed to stop in the water. Then she lifted, on a wave, and plunged forward.

"We're clear! God willed us safe!" cried Peace of God. "Had we six inches less water, we would have torn her bottom out."

Ahead now was the open sea, and the crew cheered and some of them did little jigs about the deck and shook their fists at the white water of the reefs, now receding astern. Silvers hobbled forward, took a brief look at what lay ahead, and shouted, "Tell off a man to sound the well. We may have started a plank."

He turned to Peace of God. "That was good work," he said. He glanced seaward to where the *Cerebus* was still attempting to round the rocky island, for she was too big to have tried to get through the Hell Race. "We have no need to fear her now," he added.

"No," said Peace of God soberly, "all we have to fear now is you, George Silvers."

8

We made Lynn well ahead of the *Cerebus,* anchoring just inside the harbor. As soon as the anchor was down, Captain Silvers called for a boat and went ashore, leaving the mate, Felton, to take care of the vessel.

He was gone two hours and returned with a portly gentleman most elegantly clad, whom the Maclaren pronounced a Tory as soon as he set eyes on him. This man remained for perhaps an hour aboard the brig and then departed. When he had gone the captain announced that only a few men were to remain aboard the *Betsy,* the rest having permission to go ashore and they would be paid off on the following day. This was welcome news, particularly for the highlander, who hated ships, and he, Peace of God, and I were in the first boatload to get ashore. We found Lynn a pleasant enough little town, though the harbor smelled vilely from the by-products of the shoe manufacturing which was the mainstay of the place.

The three of us were desperately hungry, for, though we had eaten aboard the brig, it had been nothing but ship's biscuits with water to wash them down, and, after our imprisonment on the barge, we craved a good meal with plenty of meat in it. But we had not a penny and, though we applied to the local militia captain for funds, it was only to be told that he had none and his own men had been unpaid for four months. He had no kitchen establishment either, where we could get a meal, but suggested that we might apply to the landlord of the Black Swan Tavern and see what he would do for us.

The Black Swan lay on a hill, a little beyond the town and on the Boston road. It was a miserable-looking place, built of fieldstones and with a hangdog air to it. The storm shutters were in danger of falling off the windows, and the stables at the back were in a state close to dilapidation. It was plain that only the most desperate travelers would ever put up at the Black Swan, and, if the food were as poor as the building, it would hardly be worth eating. We entered the front door to find a small and mean corridor with a crowded taproom off to the right. The taproom was full of smoke, both from a fire of green wood, which burned sullenly in one corner, and the pipes of the customers, of whom there were half a dozen in the room, and all of them looking as though their next stopping place would be the gallows.

"What can I do for you, gentlemen?" asked the landlord, when we had made our way to the plank, supported at each end by two barrels, which served as a bar.

"Feed us," said the Maclaren.

"You'll have a little something to pay the bill?" asked the landlord, eying our tattered clothing.

"No," said the Maclaren. "I'm a captain in the Continental Army and will gie ye my note for the money, and that should be enough for ye."

"Did you hear that now?" said the landlord to the others in the room. "He's a captain in the Continental Army and thinks he can buy food by signing a note."

But the Maclaren was no man to be trifled with in such a manner. There was a seaman standing to one side with a sheath knife in his belt. The Maclaren grabbed the landlord across the counter by the front of his shirt, and he had the seaman's knife in his hand so fast that even I did not see him take it.

"Noo," he said. "Will ye serve me food or will I serve ye steel? I'm indifferent which it is to be, for I've killed better men than you with less cause."

"You shall have food, sir," said the landlord, his face white with fright.

"Make it the best in the house," said the Maclaren, and flung him back so hard that he staggered into the wall behind the bar.

The Maclaren turned round now to survey the others in the room. "If there's any of ye take exception to my ways," he said, "ye can state yir objections now."

There was dead silence in the room while the others eyed first the Maclaren and then me and Peace of God and then each other. But none of them spoke.

The Maclaren then led the way to a table at which a man was sitting in the far corner of the room. This man was distinct from the others in that he was neatly dressed in a suit of bottle-green velvet. He was a man in his mid-twenties, his hair dark, and he was smoking a churchwarden pipe and reading a newspaper. He gave the impression of having been reading the newspaper all through the little scene before, and, when the Maclaren approached, he looked as if mildly surprised.

"I do not take any exception to your ways either," he said with a slight smile. "In fact, I welcome them. Pray be seated."

We seated ourselves around the table, and the neatly dressed gentleman introduced himself. "Putnam is my name, sirs," he said. "John Putnam. May I invite you to a glass of Madeira? 'Tis poor stuff, I'll warrant you—heavy with lees and hardly drinkable. Yet it is the best that offers in this miserable tavern."

"I would prefer rum," said the Maclaren, and introduced us.

"Did I hear you mention to our host that you are a captain of militia?" asked Mr. Putnam.

"I am," said the Maclaren, and told the story of our escape.

"A remarkable tale indeed," said Mr. Putnam. "And yet I would venture to say that she is a remarkable ship, the *Betsy*. And carries a remarkable cargo."

The Maclaren looked at him stonily but said nothing.

"Yes. A remarkable cargo. Indeed a valuable cargo. A cargo in short which should this very moment be on its way ashore, and yet I see no movement to unload it. A pity, for a few hours and it may be too late."

"What do you mean?" I asked.

"Why, sir," said Mr. Putnam, "you have eyes as good as I and must see clearly what I mean. Do you not see the *Cerebus* beyond the bar there—she is plainly visible through the window—sailing off and on and waiting for dark?"

"And what will happen when it is dark?" I asked.

"Why, I would venture to suggest that she will send in a cutting-out party in boats and take the *Betsy* and her cargo too. Not that the captain is likely to suffer, having so thoughtfully dismissed his whole crew except for a handful of men. The greater part of them will be drunk and useless by nightfall, which will make matters easier for the British boat crews."

"Ah," said Peace of God. "That would be like George Silvers. Ready money was always a sore temptation to George."

"I don't understand," I said. "There was a man aboard this morning. I took him to be the Continental agent arranging for the unloading of the cargo."

"On the contrary, I fancy he was a British agent,"

said Mr. Putnam, "with what our friend here calls ready money."

"I recall now," I said, "that it was only after this man visited the brig that the captain dismissed the crew."

"Precisely," said Mr. Putnam. He raised his glass, took a delicate sip from it, and put it down slowly on the table. "This Madeira is truly deplorable," he said.

The landlord now appeared, carrying three plates of steaming stew, which he put on the table. As he was doing so Mr. Putnam caught his eye and said gently, "You misjudged our friends here, Thomas. They are of the patriot persuasion, as they claimed."

"They have no money," grumbled the landlord.

"Which one might take as final proof of their politics," said Mr. Putnam lightly. "Pauper patriots, my good Thomas. That is what we all are. By my faith, I find it hard to blame Captain Silvers. If Thomas here found it hard to accept a note for your dinners, we are not to be surprised if Captain Silvers would find it hard to accept my note for his cargo."

"You mean that *you* are the Continental agent?" I asked, recalling all that my father had said about one pound of gunpowder now being worth a ton next year.

"I am indeed," said Mr. Putnam. "Authorized to issue a note on the Continental Congress for the purchase of the cargo of gunpowder, redeemable in ninety days. Though that is hardly to be compared with ready cash."

"It would have been better had we driven the *Betsy*

up on a reef going through the Hell Race," said Peace of God.

"Not at all," said Mr. Putnam. "For we still have a chance of getting the cargo. Though with a slightly different kind of payment."

"What kind of payment?" asked the Maclaren.

"The same you offered the landlord a moment ago. Steel. I have sent out riders to organize a boat party of my own. Half a dozen boats, I fancy, armed with fishermen would serve. But we are likely to be shorthanded. Most of the younger men from these parts are with the army at Boston. I do not suppose that you gentlemen would care to take a hand in the venture?"

"I would fight the devil on land, but I have a mortal fear of the ocean," said the Maclaren, cleaning off his plate with a hunk of bread.

"You do not impress me as a man with such reservations," said Mr. Putnam.

"To be drowned is a death for a dog," said the Maclaren.

"Come, sir," said Mr. Putnam, "I fancy you take too gloomy a view of the matter. It is after all on the cards that you might be shot or cutlassed. I fancy the figures would show that only a small portion of those engaged in sea fights are actually drowned."

But the Maclaren, having endured one ordeal upon the sea, had no stomach for another, and spoke gloomily of those traditions and sayings of his clan which pointed to disaster to the chieftains who fought upon the water.

"Well," said Mr. Putnam, "I wish only willing hearts. How about you, sir?" turning to me.

"I'm your man," I said.

"And you?" The question was addressed to Peace of God.

"I were going to see my Nancy in Salem," said Peace of God. "Yet I will come, that being where my duty lies."

"Your Nancy will be the safer for this small delay," said Mr. Putnam.

He turned now to me and said, "Are you perchance any relation of Mr. John Treegate of the Marine Committee in Boston?"

"My father went to Boston," I said, "on some special business. He did not tell me its nature."

"I fancy he is the same man," said Mr. Putnam. "He has been commissioned by the Congress to help in organizing a Continental Navy. It is no secret now. We are to have a navy, gentlemen, for this war will be won as much by sea as by land."

"But we can surely never build a navy to equal that of England," I cried.

"No," said Mr. Putnam. "We cannot. Yet your father is a vigorous man with wide powers and influence. He is such a man, I fancy, as will make a little go a long way; make a few frigates, discreetly used, the equivalent of a King's squadron. The problem is not to engage in massive sea warfare. It is rather to maintain communications with those who are likely to help us—France, for instance, and the people of Holland and their possessions in the West Indies. All with the purpose of insuring our supplies and harassing the enemy by capture of their merchantmen and supply ships."

Mr. Putnam now fished an excellent gold watch out of his fob pocket and consulted it. "Shall we agree to meet at five on the waterfront, gentlemen? Two boats will take off from here. Three will come from Cape Ann, and one more from Tedman a mile up the coast. They will rendezvous in the harbor after sunset."

"And what then?" I asked.

"Why, then we will row out to the *Betsy* with muffled oars and rowlocks, board her, and commence unloading her cargo before the British boat crew comes in."

When all was agreed, the Maclaren settled the bill by giving the landlord a piece of paper containing a promise to pay, which the landlord promptly threw in the fireplace with ill grace. Mr. Putnam then offered to settle the account with cash, but the Maclaren would not hear of it, saying he would beg a dinner from no man.

The rest of the day we spent sitting around the tavern before the fire. The Maclaren was moody, and several times suggested that we give up the idea of boarding the brig and instead return as best we could to the Continental lines outside Boston. But I would not be persuaded, and the Maclaren grew first angry and then sulky. Finally we fell asleep before the fireplace and so passed the time until sunset, when the landlord awakened us and we went down to the harbor.

We found Mr. Putnam standing on the stony beach

beside two boats. There were several men at the boats, some of them the same we had seen in the crowded tap-room of the Black Swan Tavern. There was a stack of cutlasses on the beach, which Mr. Putnam had rounded up, and a few firelocks. He had obtained the cutlasses from the captain of militia who, however, had refused to let any of his men volunteer for the venture. It was snowing again, the snow coming down in grains like sand driven by a brisk wind, and it stung our cheeks and numbed our hands. Peace of God and I took a cutlass apiece. The Maclaren picked up one also, announcing that, though he would not go with us, yet he still wished to be armed.

"Have the other boats come yet?" I asked.

"Yes," said Mr. Putnam. "They are coming in at this moment." In a few minutes four more boats had pulled up to the beach, and a man jumped out of one of them and came ashore, the remainder staying in the boats.

Now followed a short conference in which Mr. Putnam laid out his plans for attack. He proposed an assault on the brig from the shoreward side, three boats attacking up forward and three by the stern, which would divide the small crew aboard if they showed any inclination to fight.

Peace of God shook his head. "Best attack from the seaward," he said.

"Why?" asked Mr. Putnam.

"They will mistake us for the British boat party, and so George Silvers will not put up much of a fight."

"I think you're right," said Mr. Putnam.

"One thing more," said Peace of God. "Tide's on the ebb so the brig's pointed shoreward. And that's fortunate, for she's clumsy and slow in stays. But, pointed shoreward and with the wind off the sea, if we set her foretopsail we could bring her into the dock and unload her there."

"Excellent," said Mr. Putnam.

"Ah," said Peace of God, "but we must first find men that can work in the dark and shake loose the topsail. Topmost hands, we need. Four of them that can run out on the spar and loose the sail."

Four men were found and put in the same boat as Peace of God. All now being ready, the boats pushed off from the beach. The Maclaren of Spey stood irresolute on the beach. I called to him to come with us, but he would not, for he was in one of his black moods, and I left him there.

The boats divided when they were halfway out to the brig, three falling off to pass around her stern and three heading for her bow. The rowers had been instructed to keep well out of the area of light shed by the brig's lanterns. Pulling against the wind the rowers had hard work of it, though the tide was with them, and it was thirty minutes before they were all on the seaward side of the brig. Here the water was rougher, and the boats rolled and tumbled in it and were only with difficulty gotten close together so that they would come alongside the brig at about the same time.

"Give way," called Peace of God at last, and the rowers pulled with a will. Someone now moved on the deck of the brig, and ran to her forestays with a lantern and called out, "Ahoy. Who's there?"

No one replied from the boats, and the man ran to the foot of the mainmast. On the boats we could now hear the harsh, tearing sound of the battle rattle which the watchman was whirling over his head to spread the alarm. A handful of men came tumbling up on deck from the forecastle.

"Boarders away," cried Peace of God, who had now laid his boat alongside the brig. We swarmed up the futtock shrouds. Someone aboard fired a pistol, and a man close to me tumbled backward over his mate into the boat. But the rest of us came on, and a short hard scuffle took place on the deck.

It was not much of a fight and over in a minute, the skeleton crew of the brig retreating toward the waist of the ship. Here they were soon surrounded by the men from the other boats. Peace of God scrambled up the forward rigging to the foretopsail yard, followed by the topmen. Others tailed onto the foretopsail sheet and brace, and I joined a group at the capstan who were already hauling in the brig's anchor.

The brig started moving forward slowly on her anchor, and then I heard Putnam shout, "Boarders! Boarders! Throw them back."

I whirled to see a swarm of men led by a couple of lieutenants in the uniform of the Royal Navy, pouring over the sides of the brig. They had come expecting only token resistance, and found to their surprise not a skeleton crew on the brig, but twoscore tough New England fishermen, armed with cutlasses, who drove them back off the sides as fast as they had come up.

"Follow me," cried one of the lieutenants, struggling up to the gunwale of the brig. "Board her. Board her, I say." The men in the boats came on again in a swarm, and this time a couple of dozen of them cleared the gunwale at different points.

The foretopsail had now been set, but the anchor had not been broken loose. The sea wind filled the *Betsy*'s solitary sail, and she started moving forward.

I had left the capstan and flung myself at the lieutenant who was leading the boarding party. He had just pistoled a seaman and, seeing me coming, he flung the pistol at me. It struck me on the hand, knocking my cutlass to the deck. I saw the lieutenant grin, his white teeth showing clearly in his dark face, and he swung at me with his cutlass. He would have cut me to the bone, for there was no time or space to dodge, when the *Betsy* lurched heavily, throwing friend and foe in a heap on her deck. She had sailed into the dock and was now grounding her sides against it. I was on my feet before the lieutenant, and as he sought to get up drove my knee into his face and, gripping him by the shoulders, pitched him over the side. The rest of the battle was a confusion of blows given and taken in the murk of the night, and then it was over as suddenly as it had commenced. One minute we were still fighting on the deck, and the next the British had withdrawn to their boats and were pulling back toward the frigate, leaving several of their number wounded on the deck.

The precious cargo of gunpowder was safe for the time being.

Now came the task of unloading the brig, and we were hardly well started upon it when the *Cerebus* opened fire with her twenty-pounders. She was using red-hot shot, trusting that one would hit the brig, when we would all certainly be blown to pieces and half the town of Lynn as well.

It was an eerie sight to see the red-hot balls come roaring out of the blackness of the night toward us and crash into the docks and warehouses about. These balls looked like comets against the dark sky, and it was not long before they had set several buildings afire. So we had before us the task of unloading three hundred tons of gunpowder in barrels under enemy fire and with a town burning around us. It would not have been strange if the men had deserted the brig and fled to safety, for during the bombardment we lived from second to second. Yet they stayed and somehow managed to get horses and wagons in which to take the barrels of powder away from the danger zone. As soon as a wagon was full, it was driven off a mile or more inland, unloaded, and brought back for more.

The bombardment by the *Cerebus* lasted for an hour and a half, and the brig was not hit during that time. A red-hot ball was flung at us every four or five minutes, that, I suppose, being the time required to heat the ammunition. But after an hour and a half the bombardment ceased. Many buildings were burning close to the dock, and I suppose the captain of the *Cerebus* must have concluded that we had left the *Betsy* and she would shortly take fire and blow up.

Whatever the case, the frigate ceased firing and when dawn came she was not to be seen. Nor was Captain Silvers. He, I assumed, had left with the frigate, his plot to sell his cargo for cash to the British having been foiled.

There was one other person missing. The Maclaren of Spey. He had taken no hand in the unloading of the gunpowder and was not about the town. He had gone without a word of message for me.

9

Looking back on that first year of the war now, I am still surprised that we survived it—that the Revolution was not crushed and all of us who had taken part in it, from General Washington to the smallest water boy in camp, hanged or sentenced to prison for the rest of their lives.

Peace of God said that it was Divine Providence alone that sustained us, and, although I had not his religious enthusiasm, I came to believe that there was much in what he said. The odds could hardly have been heavier against us. And we, all of us, could hardly have made graver mistakes. All, then, was wrong for us and right for the enemy. And still we survived.

Take, for instance, the matter of keeping the army in the field. The Maclaren of Spey was not the only man who left us. The enlistments of the New England militia companies, who for a while formed the backbone of the army, expired. And the men, long in the field, refused to re-enlist. They went to their homes and took with them their muskets, so that we lost not merely man-power but firepower as well. At one time, until rein-forcements arrived from the other colonies, we had not sufficient men around Boston to man the entrenchments which encircled the city. Had the British known of this, they could readily have sortied from the city and cut our lines to pieces. But they did not sortie, and so we had time to rebuild our army.

Then Boston was evacuated. Up to the last minute it looked as though we would have to take the city by storm. We had brought guns down from Fort Ticonder-oga on sleds for this purpose. I, now the captain of my company in place of the Maclaren, had been given orders on the precise section of the British lines against which I was to lead my men. We rushed up gun em-placements on Dorchester Heights when our guns had arrived, and when all was ready discovered that the British had withdrawn.

The evacuation took place during the night of March 16, 1776—and on the 17th, nine months to the day from the time I had stood in the trenches of Bunker Hill awaiting the redcoat charge, we entered Boston.

That was our only triumph for almost a year. We lost New York by midsummer, and its loss was reckoned fatal to our cause. We were lucky to save the army, which was forced to flee across New Jersey into Pennsylvania. We had sent an expedition into Canada to capture Quebec, and that had been a failure too, and scarcely a third of the men who had taken part in it had returned.

And so, as 1776 drew to a close, we were camped on the field on the Pennsylvania side of the Delaware River, foodless and freezing and awaiting the final blow which would put an end to us all.

For myself, I was thoroughly heartsick, disgusted with the conduct of the army, with the inefficiency of our officers, and the continual fleeing from the enemy, from one trap into another trap, until now it seemed that we were caught in the final trap. We had the Delaware River, as I have said, between us and the enemy. But we were an army of only a few thousand, not enough to make up a division. And when the river froze, which it would do soon, the British with their German mercenaries could readily cross over and exterminate us.

What added greatly to my unhappiness was the absence without word of the Maclaren of Spey. I loved him despite all his pride and his faults. I was uneasy that he had left, not because he was out of sympathy with the cause of the Revolution, but because he had turned his back on me. This thought hurt me deeply, and many times I was tempted to leave the army as he had done and go and seek him. Perhaps the reason I stayed was because my men stayed. And perhaps the reason they remained was because I had not left. I suppose I was setting an example to them, but in reality it was they, miserable, underfed, freezing, and sick, who were setting an example to me.

And then there was always Peace of God. I had become curiously fond of him. He was gentle and yet he could be as hard as iron. He was as considerate as a woman when it came to treating the wounded, and yet I had seen him at Brooklyn Heights, when the British drove through our lines in the attack on New York, felling men with a clubbed musket as if he were killing flies and crying biblical texts as he did so. He had only one relative in the world—his daughter Nancy who was looking after his small farm for him in Massachusetts. He had been to see her once after we had saved the gunpowder on the brig *Betsy*, and he had been with me ever since.

One evening, around the middle of December, I had decided to walk up the Delaware by myself, wishing to be alone, for I was feeling particularly miserable and did not wish to talk even with Peace of God. I came to a place where there had been a barn. All that was left of it now were a few broken uprights and some rotten planks around the bottom of these. Since we were always short of firewood, I decided that I would break up some of these planks and take them back to camp, and this work might shake the mood of melancholy which settled on me more and more frequently.

While I was engaged in this task I became aware that someone was approaching from behind. Others, not trained in the wilderness, would not have known this, but my hearing was acute. I stopped what I was doing and slipped behind what remained of the wall of the barn and waited. Presently a tall man, wearing a cocked hat and clad in a cloak, came and stood by the river, looking intently at the water as it flowed past. He picked up a stone, tossed it into the current, and I heard the crashing sound it made as it penetrated the skin of ice which nightly formed on the river. Then he squatted down beside the river, staring across it.

I decided that for sport I would give him a fright, and so crept up behind him, which was very easy to do, for the man was plainly lost in thought and I could move very quietly. When I was directly behind him I said in a low voice, "If you make one move, you are a dead man."

"You are quite wrong, my friend," said the stranger without turning. "The position is precisely the opposite. If I do not move, I am dead. The point is, what move to make?"

"I would advise sitting where you are until I release you," I said. "What you feel in your back is a knife and I am a man who can use it."

"Are you of the Continental Army?" the man asked.

"I am," I replied.

"So am I," said the man. "May I get up? I am getting a cramp squatting here."

"Yes," I said. "But first tell me who you are?"

"General Washington," said the man, rising slowly and then turning to face me. He stood higher than I, but not much, for I was close to six feet, and when I saw his face I knew he was not lying. He had the prominent nose, flat strong jaw, dark eyebrows, and high cheekbones of the Commander-in-Chief of the Continental Army. I had seen him several times, and close too, but never as close as this.

I was not flustered by finding that the man I had surprised was my commander-in-chief. Despite my years, I was no boy to be embarrassed in the presence of a big man but had seen a great deal more of living than many men twice my age, so I looked him over boldly and then smiled.

"Had you not turned around," I said, "I believe I would have guessed that you were Washington."

"How so?" he asked softly.

"Because you are so unwary," I said. "You stroll unguarded along the river and are throwing stones in the water when I come upon you and make you my prisoner. Had I been one of the Hessians or the British, you would have been dead."

"And you think this my natural behavior?" he asked, without a trace of anger.

"To be plain about it, yes," I replied. "You are a man who is unaware of traps. You had the army in a trap on Manhattan Island with the British in command of the river, and then on Long Island, and now you have us in a trap here and are waiting for the door to shut —or in other words for the river to freeze, so that the Hessians can come over and clean us up."

He laughed ruefully. "It is plain you do not think much of my generalship," he said. "And you are right. I have made a number of blunders. And I expect I will make more, though seeking to avoid them. But you must be lenient, for my profession is not that of a general. I am called upon to exercise that which I am still learning."

I had expected him to be annoyed at my plain talk, but instead he was humble and that humility won me over to him immediately. Indeed, I felt a bit ashamed of myself. I sensed that here was a man who was not too great to learn, or too proud to admit fault. I found myself, at that moment, most anxious to be of any service I could to him.

"You are from the frontier?" he asked, looking at my costume.

"Yes," I replied.

"Tell me, being from the frontier, do you know anything about rivers in wintertime?"

"Something," I replied, not sure what he was driving at.

"This river here," he said, "is it ready to freeze?"

"Yes," I said. "The ground is frozen. The upper reaches of the river are frozen. The blocks of ice which are moving down in it now from upstream will soon jam in the river, and that will trap the water hereabout.

And as soon as it is trapped or slowed by the ice jams, then the river will freeze."

"That is what I have been thinking myself," said Washington. "It will freeze. And once it freezes it will be possible to move an army with cannon across it. And there is no way to prevent its freezing. The river was my shield a few weeks ago. In a few days it will turn into a trap." He smiled wryly. "I have a kind of genius for getting into traps, as you have said. I must develop a genius for getting out of them."

He now pulled aside his cloak and, producing a silver whistle, blew a single note on it. Immediately several figures carrying rifles converged on us, out of the darkness.

"You see, my friend," said Washington, pointing to the men who now stood around us. "You had not trapped me at all. It was I who had trapped you." And with that he sent me back to my camp (under escort less it should turn out that I was really a spy), and I learned a good lesson from a man who I found was more cunning than I thought.

The next week proved so cold that I excused the forty men of my company from any outside duties which were not essential. There was no snow—it was too cold to snow. But the skies were a heavy gray from horizon to horizon, and the earth as hard as iron. There were a great many ruts around our encampment, made in the mud when the weather had been milder, and these now froze into ridges as hard as iron and cut the men's feet.

Many of my men had no shoes. Nor had they anything out of which to make shoes. They tied rags around their feet and stuffed straw inside the rags, but that kind of footwear was useless for walking on the saw-toothed edges of frozen mud around the camp. My own moccasins had long gone, and I was barefooted myself, but more used to it than my men, who had been brought up in civilized parts.

We had calked our huts against the wind, but they were overcrowded and full of lice. Bedclothes had long ago been turned into cloaks and coats and even trousers and gaiters. The scraps were used for footwear. We had made bunks in the huts, but these had now been chopped up for firewood. I drew from the quartermaster each day ten pounds of flour for my forty men, and sometimes got a piece of salt beef. Occasionally we got a few potatoes, but this diet was hardly enough to maintain the men in health, and we went from day to day in this fashion, always cold, always hungry, and, because of the cold and hunger, sleepless.

What bothered me most was that the men were anxiously looking forward to the end of their enlistment. The enlistment of half the men in my company expired December 31.

On the first of the month one of the men started to cut notches on the corner post of one of the huts, marking the expiration of the days until the time when he and many others would be free to leave the army and go back to their homes. As the weather grew colder, the men took also to watching the river, and a kind of contest in which the stakes were life and liberty versus death took place.

The problem, simply put, was, would the Delaware freeze over and the Hessians attack before the men's time expired? All the discussion in the huts centered around this question, for, if the river froze before the end of December, men who might expect to be free of army life and comfortably restored to their families would instead be either killed or taken prisoner.

This was the situation when orders came to parade in full battle equipment, down by a ferry across the Delaware called McKonkey's. We got these orders on Christmas Day, or rather the evening of Christmas Day—a day marked by a bitter wind from the northeast which brought with it first rain, then snow, then sleet, and then more sleet, so that the men had stayed in their huts except those who had had sentry duty. The orders came as a surprise to all of us, but not one man of my company grumbled or uttered a word of resistance.

They staggered out of the huts into the sleet in their rags, some of them with their faces muffled with bits of sacking as protection from the weather, some bareheaded, and their long hair whipping to rat tails about them. I walked along with them carrying a lantern, checking their muskets, and I was proud that so many of them had taken a piece of rag from their clothing and wrapped it around the lock of their muskets to keep the firing pan dry. One of the men—the one in fact who had been most anxious about seeing that a notch was cut each day on the post of the hut—stopped me as I went by.

"What's happening, Cap'n?" he asked.

"I think we're going to cross the river and attack," I said.

"Pity we didn't attack earlier," he said.

"Why?" I asked, very surprised.

"We could have shared their Christmas dinner," was the reply, and the squad started laughing at the thought.

We got orders to move in single file down to the river, and here there was a great deal of confusion. About a score of heavy boats had been collected along the bank, and men, horses, and artillery pieces were being loaded into these in what might be termed half a gale. The wind whistled and shrieked around us, and the sleet stung our hands and faces. The boats rocked and swung in the river with ice floes thumping against their sides, while the oarsmen aboard struggled to keep them to the shore while they were being loaded. Horses whinnied, men shouted, guns were manhandled up narrow planks to thump into the bottom of the boats, and orders and counterorders were shouted in the darkness above the whining of the wind.

It was two hours after we reached the river's edge that we got aboard the boats. There was some argument among the command about whether the artillery should be taken over first or last, and this caused considerable delay. Eventually it was decided that the guns should go over with the men, and the twenty-pounders, some of them off ships in the river, were dumped into the boats with us.

They were so heavy they upset the trim of the boats and added enormously to the labors of the fishermen from Maine, who manned the craft. The boat in which I made the crossing of the Delaware was so badly out of trim that we had to jettison a score of twenty-pound shot in midstream to escape being swamped. One boat foundered close by to us, and the men, struggling in the water, grabbed the sides of our vessel and almost swamped us. But somehow we got to the other side, every one of us soaking wet. And once we were there we had to wait again in the freezing wind while the rest of the army got across.

By now all knew our objective. We were to attack Trenton, about nine miles' march from the point where we landed. The attack was to be made at dawn. The troops had been moved from Pennsylvania to the New Jersey bank of the Delaware by three in the morning, and when we got orders to march, I saw Washington move forward to the head of the column, mounted on a white horse.

"Well," I said to myself, "you have us out of one trap, but it is still to be seen whether you have not put us in another."

10

Our orders were that we were to march in complete silence, and that no man was to speak above a whisper or to fall out of the line on pain of death. The wheels of the cannon had been muffled with blankets, or rather the shreds of blankets, and their axles greased to reduce the noise from them. We had not sufficient horses or mules to pull them, and so men were given this task, tailing onto ropes from the axles. The storm did not abate for one minute, but mercifully it was from behind us as we took the road to Trenton. When we had gone a little way our army was split in two, one detachment being ordered to go along the shore of the Delaware, and another (to which I was assigned) to strike a couple of miles inland. The effect was that we would attack the city from two points, one in the southeast and the other in the northwest, and join forces somewhere in the center of Trenton.

Washington led the division to which I was attached, riding at the head of the column, with my own company immediately behind him and his officers. Many of my men were straggling, for they were not in a condition to march even in fair weather, and this was as foul a night as could be imagined. One fellow fell several times in half a mile, and Peace of God took his musket from him. But the man, even lightened of the burden, was not up to the task. So I hoisted him on my own back and carried him thus for perhaps a quarter of a mile. Then, a halt being called for a few minutes, I put him down and he lay on the ground without a word or a movement. I spoke to him and he did not answer. He had died of the cold.

There was dawn in the east as we circled Trenton to get to our attacking position in the rear. As we approached the city we halted once more, and orders were passed along our column to charge and prime our muskets. While I was seeing to this among the men of my company, a colonel came to me and said that I was to take the company forward of the main body and search for enemy pickets or cannon. If there were pickets, I was to drive them in, but if I ran into a heavy em-placement of cannon I was to fall back, when the main column would come to my relief.

I took my men out of the road, deploying them on both sides of it in open order and went forward toward the city, whose rooftops we could see now dimly through the storm. We came to a solitary house in which there was no sign of occupation or anyone to be seen outside. Then I saw a slight movement in the doorway, no more than a shifting of a shadow, as it were, but it was enough for me. I took aim and fired, and the next minute a dozen Hessians came pouring out of the door and through the windows of the house. Some of them were in their nightshirts. They opened fire hastily in our direction, and we fired back quick and hot when they fled in the direction of the town.

That started the attack. There was a roar from my men, and we gave chase across garden fences and down little alleyways. Windows were thrown open and then slammed shut all around us. Hens scattered in clouds, dogs barked and yowled, and then from the other side of the town we heard the noise of heavy firing and the report of a cannon.

The rest of our detachment had now come down the road, which became, as it entered the town, the principal street of Trenton. We plunged into a square from which several streets gave off and found it full of Hessians, who to the rattle of drums and the blaring of bugles were attempting to form up.

They got no opportunity to do so.

There was a volley from our men, and the Hessians

went down in the snow of the square. Others meanwhile were pouring out of the barracks, their officers roaring encouragement at them. There were several cannon before the barracks, and two of these were wheeled quickly forward and turned to point at us.

Many of us had gained the open area of the square and were firing into the Hessians, but the rest were still bottled up in the street by which we had entered the town. Seeing the cannon pointed at them, those in the forefront of our lines in the street panicked, for one round from the cannon would have cut a path lined with dead men. They shouted to go back and, since those behind were still pressing forward, a terrible struggle took place for a moment in our own ranks. Meanwhile, some of the Hessians had managed to form lines, but they were impeded by their own men, who were moiling about before them.

"Get that gunner," someone shouted.

I caught a glimpse of a man at the mouth of one of the cannon ramming home the charge. The range was short—only fifty paces—and I shot from the hip, and he collapsed over the gun. But another had soon taken his place. I snatched a musket from the man nearest me and fired again. That shot missed. Several others fired now, but the gunner had a charmed life, for he got the charge rammed home without being hurt, and a man at the breech brought up a flaming torch to put to the touchhole of the cannon and fire the piece.

It was Peace of God who saved us.

He flung something heavy, which caught the gunner

in the face and sent him staggering back, just as he was about to put the burning torch to the touchhole. Then we rushed the gun, going in with the bayonet, and had captured it in a second. We dragged it around to face the Hessians at the other side of the square, and they, seeing themselves looking straight into its barrel, broke for cover. But an officer cried out to some of the men to follow him. They were tall fellows in leather gaiters and queer, squarish leather hats, and I later discovered they were the select grenadiers of the garrison. They rushed behind their officer at the cannon. They were almost upon it when we fired, and when the smoke had cleared away hardly one of the grenadiers was left and their officer lay dying among them.

Still the day was not won.

Another gun was brought by the Hessians down a side street and fired, though I did not see that it did any damage. A column of their men had been got together hurriedly in a smaller square adjoining the one in which the main action took place, and now charged at us. They were met with a storm of bullets, but still came on so that we were driven back across the square and lost possession of the cannon which we had captured. Then, when it seemed that we were likely to be driven out of Trenton by the road by which we had entered, the other division of our army, which had been fighting on the outskirts, burst into the center of the town and all was over in a few seconds. Seeing us so heavily reinforced, the Hessians threw down their muskets and surrendered. We thrust them into houses and barracks and locked them in there, and went about mopping up the few groups which still resisted.

From start to finish the action had lasted little over twenty minutes.

Immediately the last resistance had been overcome, I got together my company at one end of the square and, putting them under the command of Peace of God, told him to keep them there while I took ten men and foraged for food. None of my company had eaten what could be described as a meal for a week, and I was certain that the Hessians had been well supplied with food for their Christmas—indeed a number of those who had fallen in the battle were still half intoxicated from the previous day's revels.

"See if you can find my Bible," said Peace of God, as I was about to leave.

"Your Bible?" I cried.

"Yes," said the fisherman. "It was with it that I brought down the gunner who was about to fire the cannon. I had nothing else handy to throw, and I trust that God will forgive me." He seemed genuinely wretched at the use to which he had put his volume of Scripture, and I knew he would not be comforted unless the Bible were found, which he would take as a sign of forgiveness for his action.

I assured him gravely that I would look for it, and, as it was, found it readily enough. It was a thick but small volume, bound by a heavy clasp and weighing about a pound and a half. It was not damaged, and I put it in my tunic and set about my search for food.

Food was not hard to find. There was plenty of it in the kitchen of the barracks, and the cooks had just been preparing breakfast for the soldiers of the garrison, so that it was hot as well. I got several bowls of porridge and some lengths of blood and liver sausages, five loaves of bread, and a quantity of other food, including two hams. These I sent to the men of my company with orders that half were to eat while the other half stood by, for I was fearful that we would be attacked once more. I believe that what inspired this feeling was a conviction that, though we had won a victory, we were still in a trap. And so we were. We were in enemy territory, cut off by the river from our communication with Philadelphia, and General Washington, in my view, was famous for getting his army trapped.

I did not eat with the men myself, but decided that I ought to get into the officers' quarters and, nervous as I was about our position in Trenton, search through what papers I could find which would give some indication of the placement of the enemies' forces.

Accordingly I left the barracks and went to a house, where I learned that a few British officers, attached to the Hessians for liaison purposes, had been housed. This house, up to the present, had been neglected by those who were searching the town.

The door was open and there was no one in the downstairs rooms. I found one which had served as a study and started pulling the drawers out of a desk, hoping to find some orders or correspondence which might be useful. There was little enough to be found—

two snuffboxes, several decks of cards, all well used, a bill from a smith in New York for "a dress sword, chased upon the blade," and a few sheets of paper with figures on them which I took to be the tally of some card game. I turned to a large cupboard in the room. Here I found four excellent pairs of boots and was putting one pair on when I caught a glimpse of a portrait on the wall opposite which startled me and brought back a rush of memories and filled me with a sense of guilt.

The portrait was a large one and showed a man of perhaps thirty years in a green military jacket, which I knew to be the uniform of the Rifle Brigade of the British Army. The face was toward me and seemed to be examining me with a slight smile. The chin was supported in the right hand of the sitter, and on the middle finger of this hand was a heavy silver ring. Set in the center of the ring was a stone which I recognized immediately. It was precisely the same stone which the Maclaren of Spey had worn in the tara brooch which marked him as chief of his clan.

It was almost a year since the Maclaren had left me, and in that time my sense of loss at his going away had diminished. But the sight of the stone in that ring brought back to me, with overwhelming force, my loneliness. I recalled the many kindnesses he had shown me, the care he had taken of me in the wilderness when I had been sick, how once he had saved my life from a bear and how he had taught me to shoot and to fight and taught me also all the woodcraft which I knew. The stone seemed to me to be a call to return to him, for he was in need of my help. It was almost as if I could hear his voice and see him surrounded by enemies, waiting for me, whom he had taken as a son and the last of his clan, to come to him.

I sprang from the chair and strode to the portrait to examine it more closely. Whoever the artist, he had painted the stone in the ring with such care and exactness that it seemed I might almost pluck it off the canvas.

On the frame of the picture at the bottom was a name-plate with on it the wording:

Maurice Pett, Esq.,
CAPTAIN, His Majesty's Rifle Brigade

Pett! The name was immediately familiar, for it was Sir John Pett who had spared me and the Maclaren from hanging when we had been captured during the siege of Boston a year before. I recalled that he had been interested in the Maclaren's brooch at that time, and had asked him whether there might be another one like it. The man in the portrait, then, must be Sir John's son. And, no doubt, during Sir John's campaigning thirty years before in the Scottish Highlands, he had come upon this stone, taken a fancy to it, and had it mounted in a ring and given it to his son.

All this seemed reasonable enough, for stranger things have happened in war. Yet the stone seemed to have a message for me, and that message plainly that I must return to my foster father. The Maclaren had told me many times that, when the chieftain wished to summon any distant member of the clan, he sent the brooch with the stone in it, and this was a summons which must never be neglected. Indeed, he had said that in the past the stone and brooch had miraculously appeared to distant members of the clan summoning them back again to their chieftain in time of crisis. It was plain to me that this was what was happening now—for the stone was clearly before me and I knew that I must return to my foster father.

I left the house in great agitation, and, pausing at the door for one more glance at this singular portrait, it seemed that the stone glowed brightly in the canvas and that the face of the sitter was mocking me and daring me to answer its call. I was greatly shaken and glad to get out of the house into the street, even though the weather had worsened, and the predawn sleet had turned to a storm of hailstones.

We quit the town late that afternoon, returning to the farther side of the Delaware. We were greatly handicapped by war prisoners, of whom we had taken about a thousand. Indeed they made up 50 per cent of our own force and added to them were the muskets, cartridges, guns, and other stores which were part of our spoils. So we were many hours getting back over the Delaware, and all the time, at the back of our minds, was the thought that the enemy, hearing of our raid, would mass and attack us, for there were heavy enemy detachments at Princeton.

But eventually we gained the Pennsylvania shore and camped that night in the field.

That night I dreamed of the Maclaren of Spey. I saw him standing alone in a rocky valley, surrounded by dead men and calling to me to help him. The following morning I had resolved to ask leave of my colonel and go to the Carolinas and seek the Maclaren, for I was convinced that he was in desperate need of my aid.

I consulted with Peace of God about it, and he said that it would be proper for me to cast "*sortes*" in the Bible, by which I would find what I was to do. He therefore took his Bible, gave it to me, bade me shut my eyes, open the book, and put my finger, still with my eyes shut, on the opened page.

The verse on which my finger rested was the twenty-second of the thirty-second chapter of Ezekiel and read, "Asshur is there and all his multitude; their graves are about him, all of them slain . . ."

When I had read this I determined that I must leave and find the Maclaren, and in this Peace of God agreed and said he would come with me.

11

My application for leave, which I made to my colonel within the hour, was turned aside with anger.

"Are you out of your mind?" he stormed at me. "Have you forgotten that the enlistment of 50 per cent of your company expires in five days' time, and that within sight and sound of the enemy this army is likely to dwindle to less than a couple of thousand men, unless others can be persuaded to enlist? Great heavens, man! Have you lost all sense of duty to your country? Get back to your men and do not let me hear another word about this matter."

The alternative was to desert and I planned to do so, leaving the lines that evening. What prevented me was not fear of capture and execution. I had gone a quarter of a mile on my way when I remembered the man I had carried on my back during the march on Trenton. When I put him down he had been dead of cold, but he had been faithful to the end. I turned and walked back to our encampment, determined to stay at least until the strength of the army had been restored.

So, far from leaving myself, I had to turn to persuading the men of the company to remain for a few more weeks until they could be replaced by fresh levies. In all this time I was in an agony of mind, because of the call of the stone, and I had little success with my men.

The men told me plainly that they considered they had done their duty to the fullest and would not stay a day more than required by regulations. And it was the same with most of the other companies. We were authorized to make promises of increased pay. But these promises were openly laughed at. The men had not even drawn the pay to which they were already entitled. They had letters from their wives complaining that the paper money sent home was held worthless for the paying of rent or the purchase of food. "Not worth a continental" was the phrase which was current at the time, and it adequately expressed the public opinion of continental currency.

Finally, since so few were prepared to re-enlist, the troops were paraded and addressed by Washington himself. A few of the phrases he used in his address have remained with me and I give them now, as I remember them.

"We have won a great victory at Trenton," he said, "and put to rout a strongly entrenched, well-armed, and superior force of the enemy after a night's march which few soldiers in any army in the world would undertake. You are, many of you now, looking forward to a well-earned reunion with your wives and your families, from whom you have long been separated, and always in danger of your lives. It grieves me deeply that I must ask you to forgo this and remain a few weeks more with your colors. But your services are more critically needed in the month that lies ahead, until further recruits can be had, than perhaps in any month since the beginning of the war. I am asking you as your Commander-in-Chief, and one who has ever had your best interests in my heart, to volunteer for a further month. That is all I ask of you. Let each man who accedes to this plea step forward from the ranks when the drum is sounded."

He fell quiet then and a roll was beaten upon the drums. But I am ashamed to say that not a single man stepped forward. The ranks remained immobile.

Washington tried once more, his face flushed, and yet he showed no sign of anger.

"My brave fellows," he said, "you have done all I asked you to do, and more than could be reasonably expected; but your country is at stake, your wives, your houses, and all that you hold dear. You have worn yourselves out with fatigues and hardships but we know not how to spare you. If you will consent to stay only one month longer, you will render that service to the cause of liberty and to your country which you probably never can do under any other circumstance."

Again there was a roll upon the drums, and this time several men, moved by the last address of their general, which he gave with a quiet dignity rather than any great eloquence, stepped from the ranks. They were soon followed by others, and Washington, seeing these ragged fellows, some of them wounded, volunteer for service, doffed his hat and bowed deeply to them in the saddle. An aide inquired whether the names of the men who had volunteered should be taken and entered on the muster roll of the New Year.

"No," said Washington. "I do not need a muster roll of men such as these to keep them to their duty."

The following day I received five pounds in silver to distribute among those of my men who had volunteered for further service, and made the distribution. Most of the men asked whether the money might not be sent to their families as they had no need of it, and I arranged with the paymaster for this to be done.

We now crossed the Delaware once more in what seemed to me a move of utter foolishness. We took up positions to the east of Trenton, facing the city across the Assanpink Creek, and the British, under Cornwallis, had soon come up with us and opened a furious fire with cannon at our positions. We had brought over cannon also, and the artillery exchange continued until dusk while we labored to put up better entrenchments and wondered why, when we had been perfectly safe across the Delaware, we should have invaded the territory of a thoroughly aroused enemy.

The men were in a bad mood and so was I. They felt that they had been cajoled into re-enlisting and now their lives were to be thrown worthlessly away, and that by morning our position would be stormed by a superior force of the British against whom we had no hope of standing. Nor could we again retreat across the Delaware. The ice was so thick that it had taken us two days to get over, and in any case our boats had been sent down the river toward Burlington with our baggage.

About nine that evening, having called on my colonel on some matter concerning the strengthening of our position, I was asked what I thought of the situation and gave vent to my feelings in plain language, saying that we were in a trap and I could see no reason for our having put ourselves in such a predicament.

"You may be surprised to learn then," said the colonel, "that we are about to get out of this trap."

"Oh," said I.

"Yes," said the colonel. "For in a little while we will have stolen away toward Princeton, and when Cornwallis attacks in the morning he will find that we are several miles away and on his left flank, between him and his base."

And so it turned out. Around midnight we got orders to quit our positions but leave our campfires burning bright. A few volunteers were asked to stay behind and give the appearance of continuing to work on the entrenchments, making a noise with spades and pickaxes, while we, as silent as an army of ghosts, stole in column up a road heading roughly north toward Princeton.

At about dawn we were within sight of the spire of Princeton church when a horseman appeared on a hill over to our left. He had gone in a second, and then from ahead there came a tattered explosion of musketry which increased with each second, so that I knew we had run into a strong body of the enemy. We immediately deployed from the road across a field, and were hardly in position before the enemy charged, coming at us with the bayonet. We gave them three rounds and then retired, for we had no bayonets in our company. Then Washington appeared, bringing up another brigade. "Stand firm," he shouted. "Stand firm. There is but a handful of them."

On he galloped into the smoke of the battle, and, having now had a moment to reload, we followed him. We got somehow into an orchard, and here a heavy battle took place between us and a couple of remnants of the enemy. They charged twice and were repelled twice and, coming at us once again, some cannon to our rear opened fire with grape and shattered them. Then we drove forward across a bridge into Princeton, and the fighting now took place from street to street and house to house. Some of the troops of the enemy wore the green uniform of the British Rifle Brigade, and the sight of this uniform startled me even in the excitement of the battle. A group of them were firing from the protection of a farm cart which had been pulled across a street. I caught a glimpse of the officer in charge of them. He was the same man whose portrait I had seen in the house in Trenton. We both fired at each other in the same moment. His bullet struck me in the side of the face, and I fell to the ground. Peace of God pulled me to the side of the street.

"That officer," I cried. "The one in the green tunic. Get him."

I pushed Peace of God aside and ran back to the street. The officer was still on the wagon. He saw me running toward him and fired again. There was a searing pain in my shoulder, and I tumbled to the ground and lost consciousness.

When I came to my senses, I was lying on some straw and Peace of God was bending over me.

"The green officer," I said. "Was he killed?"

"You have been raving about him for two days," said Peace of God. "What is he to you?"

"I do not know," I replied. "But he had a ring with the Maclaren's stone in it."

"You have been raving about that too," was the reply. "And also quoting Ezekiel, chapter thirty-second, verse the twenty-second, as follows: 'Asshur is there, and all his multitude; their graves are about him, all of them slain. . . .'"

"I must find the Maclaren," I said and, feeling suddenly very weak, fell asleep.

I was two weeks getting well enough to take any stock of my position. The ball which had wounded me in the side of the face had chipped my cheekbone and plowed a furrow below my ear to the back of my neck. The wound, however, was not as serious as the one to my shoulder. This had smashed the bone of my upper arm just below the joint and, until the bone knitted again, I would have to have my arm immobilized to my side.

I inquired where I was when I had sufficient wit to do so, and learned that the army had gone to Morristown and I was in a hut which served as a hospital there. Hearing that I was out of my delirium, my colonel came to visit me and said I might have either a discharge or a leave of absence, whichever I preferred. I asked him whether I might have a leave of some months' duration, and he said that he could arrange this.

I was several weeks regaining my strength and was in a turmoil of anxiety to be gone in all that time. Peace of God stayed with me, patiently nursing me back to health. My father visited me twice. He looked much older than the day we had stood together in the trench at Breed's Hill and seemed very preoccupied. He would talk little about his business, which seemed to be of the most secret kind, but toward the end of our last talk together said that matters were desperate for our cause.

"It is certain that Howe will attack Philadelphia," he said, "and certain too that we can hardly expect to hold it. We are not strong enough to fight this war alone and must have help."

"From whom can we get help?" I asked.

"From France," he replied. "If we could this summer achieve one great victory—destroy or receive the surrender of a British army, that would do the trick. The French sympathize with us. But they hold aloof, feeling that we have taken on more than we can accomplish. The victories at Trenton and Princeton enormously advanced our cause in France. But they are not enough. We need one great victory—one complete surrender on the part of the British, and then we will no longer be fighting alone. The French will certainly come in."

"We will never achieve such a victory," I said. "When it comes to a surprise raid on a British detachment we do well. But in the open field we are no match for the British and Hessians. We are not trained to fight in that way and never will be. Our kind of fighting demands the sort of territory that the English won't venture into —the wilderness."

"The wilderness," said my father. "That is where you were brought up. And that is why I am talking to you on this subject now. What are you planning to do when you recover from your wounds?"

I did not want to tell him, knowing that there was no love lost between my father and the Maclaren of Spey. But I had no practice in deceit and so said that I was determined to find the highlander, for I had for some weeks had a growing feeling that he was in peril. I told him about the portrait of the green officer wearing the stone of the Maclaren and that I was convinced that this was a summons for me to return to him.

"You are caught between two worlds," said my father when I had done. "You are trapped between the ancient world of the feuds and loyalties of the clans of Scotland and the modern world where clans no longer matter; nations have taken their place. You cannot keep switching from one to the other. You must make a plain choice—either to be an American whose duty is to this country, or to be a member of a Scottish clan where your duty would be to the leader of the clan—in this case the Maclaren of Spey.

"That man saved your life and brought you up. For that I will be eternally grateful to him. But he is an evil influence on you. Having saved your life, he has convinced you that he owns your life—that he may order it around as he pleases. He would draw you into his background, which is a feudal background completely foreign to this country and to all the principles for which it stands. You cannot continue in this manner. You must either go to the Maclaren and continue with him in the wilderness leading the life of feudal Scotland, or you must serve your country in the cause of the freedom of all men."

"Do I indeed have to make such a decision?" I asked.

"Yes," said my father. "You have to make it. You must go one way or the other. You must decide whether you are of the clan of Maclaren or of the nation of America. You cannot be both."

"And if I go to the Maclaren, does it mean that I have parted from you?"

My father was a stern and uncompromising man. He got up from the chair in which he had been sitting and went to the door of the hut and stood for some time looking out of it. Then he turned and said, "If you go to the Maclaren, you are not my son any longer."

I suppose the words should have saddened me but they did not. They angered me. There was the threat of disinheriting me, and I had been raised to resent threats.

"Very well then," I said stiffly, "I am no longer Peter Treegate. I am the kinsman of the Maclaren of Spey and I will go to him." I had hardly uttered the words before I repented them, but I was too proud to admit it. For a moment we faced each other across the hut, my father's face white with grief and strain. But he was proud also and said, "Very well. As you wish." And he went out of the door.

So I left the Continental Army and went to the Carolinas to seek the Maclaren. Peace of God came with me, taking only his Bible. I told him nothing of my parting with my father and he asked no questions. Indeed, in the journey to the valley which the Maclaren claimed as his own domain, I recall no conversation at all with Peace of God.

And when I found the Maclaren in the hut fort which he had built at the head of the valley and in which he had raised me as a boy, I said to him, "I have come back to you."

He was skinning the forequarters of a deer, and although I knew he had seen me approach along the floor of the valley for upward of an hour he went on with his task, merely saying, "Ye stayed long away." But I knew that he was glad I had returned, for he would look at me and smile knowingly, and when we had eaten and he had drunk a pannikin of rum, the spirits streaming down his beard, so fast did he swallow it, he threw the pannikin aside and said, "I knew ye would come back, Peter. We are the last of the Maclarens, you and I, and the clan mustna' die oot. I hae it in me mind that ye should wed ane o' the Fraser women. They are kin of ours and raise guid sons."

12

I had forgotten during the service in the Continental Army the solemn beauty of the wilderness. I had been long in the farmlands of New England, where all the land had been reduced to prettiness by tilling. But in the Maclaren's valley the very savageness of the country filled me with delight. Here were mountains on whose sides were boulders, many of which were larger than the biggest house in the city of Boston. The bottom of the valley was a tangle of forest, mostly pines. The pines grew so close together in places that it was not possible to squeeze between their trunks. Some of them were over a hundred feet in height. I delighted to climb to their tops, where the thickness of the trunk was little more than that of my own leg, and feel the tree swaying gently beneath me while I looked about through the green branches and up at the great sky. I felt at such times that I was part of the forest and of the sky, and this brought me great peace.

The valley was the Maclaren's. It was about twelve miles long, and from mountain wall to mountain wall about five miles. None entered it without his permission. For him it replaced that wild valley in Scotland where he had lived before the rising of '45. Here he planned, through me, to restore his clan. The valley being his, then it was also mine, my own heritage from which it was my duty to keep out strangers.

There were many members of the Scottish clans in these valleys. In the one adjoining ours were the Frasers —five men and eight women and four boys. At the end of the valley over a small saddle were the Campbells of Bungurrin. On our right were the Farquesons. In all I suppose there were about three hundred men from the Scottish Highlands in the valleys about, all of them loyal to the House of Stuart, which had not occupied the English throne now for ninety years. I was living not in the present but in the past. I knew that what I was trying to do was to revive the past and give it continuance in the future; to restore Scotland in the heart of America, and for a while this prospect pleased me.

In the Maclaren's valley it was as if no war was being waged in the New England States almost a thousand miles from us. All that seemed remote and unreal. What was real was that the Campbells had a blood feud of two hundred years' standing with the Farquesons and that the Maclarens were allies of the Campbells and therefore enemies of the Farquesons.

This blood feud was explained to me in detail, and I give it now as an illustration of the motivation of the highlanders.

It seems that two hundred years previously, when the two clans had been friendly, a Farqueson and a Campbell had been in love with the same girl. The Farqueson had visited the Campbell and the two men had gone hunting together, having agreed that whoever secured the best trophy should be free to press his suit, the other rival dropping out of the contest.

After a few days the two young men had returned and each had as his trophy an excellent stag's head. It was impossible to decide which was the better, and so they had gone off again. Once more they returned and once more it was impossible to decide between the merits of the trophies. The full telling of this tale took an entire evening, for they were five times bringing back trophies, and each episode of hunting was made into a saga of its own.

The sixth time Farqueson alone returned. "I have the best trophy," he cried, "and none of you will be able to dispute it." He opened his game bag and flung on the floor the head of the rival Campbell.

This savage episode had occurred, as near as I could tell, around 1550. It was still the cause of the bad blood between the Campbells and Farquesons.

One day I met one of the Farqueson men among the rocks at the top of the mountain which divided our territory from theirs. There was a sort of no man's land here. I had gone there to take in the view and, the climb being steep, had left my rifle farther down the slope. The Farqueson had his rifle with him.

"Good day to you, Peter Run Away," he said. "You are feeling bold this morning." The taunt, I knew, was directed at my leaving the Continental Army.

"Why bold?" I asked.

"You have left your valley where the old man protects you from the redcoats," he sneered.

"You speak bravely, having a rifle," I said. "But if I had mine, you would not talk so loud."

"I have a mind to see you run, Peter Run Away," he said. "Now run for me," and with that he picked up his rifle and aimed it at me. There was a boulder nearby and I ducked behind it, for I knew this man was murderous. He stepped a little to the side and fired and the ball grazed my hand. "Come," he cried, "run for me."

I flung myself at him but my arm was not well healed at this time. The bone had knitted but the muscles were weak and he knew this. He seized my wrist and pulled my arm behind me, thrusting it up toward the middle of the back until I was sure that the newly knit bone would part again.

"Say you are afraid of the redcoats and so left the war," he demanded.

I gritted my teeth but said nothing. He jerked my arm up even farther so that the agony brought out the sweat on my face.

"Come," he said, "say you ran from the redcoats."

At that moment there was a report and the Farqueson staggered back, clutching his arm.

"I followed thee," said Peace of God, reloading the rifle from which he had fired. "Thou art surrounded by devils in these parts and should return to the company of goodly men whose cause is righteous."

The Farqueson went off cursing, and I returned with Peace of God to our valley and decided to say nothing of my meeting with our foe. Peace of God did not speak during our return. But thereafter I sensed a coldness on the part of the other highlanders toward me, and the Maclaren became more moody with me if that were possible.

Toward the middle of June increasing news of the war being fought hundreds of miles away began to drift into the valleys. We got most of our news from the Indians, who were always traveling about and in touch with neighboring tribes, so that there was a chain of communication among them which far exceeded anything among the whites. It seemed that a big British force was striking down from Canada along the valley of the Hudson, the objective being Albany. Washington was miles away, attempting to save Philadelphia from Howe, and so it was plain to us that the British would soon hold the whole of New York State, cutting off the northern colonies from the south and speedily bringing the war to a close.

We did not get all this information of course from the Indians. All they knew was that the British were invading from Canada and hiring Indians to take them through the wilderness.

The rest I figured out for my own edification and that of the Maclaren, drawing a map of the area and speculating on the British route.

The Maclaren initially was not much interested, but when I had made a good map on a piece of deerhide, filling in some of the detail with the aid of Peace of God, who knew the northern colonies well, he became enthralled. He had rarely before seen a map, let alone seen a campaign laid out on it. Indeed he had no idea what a campaign was. War for him meant battles, fought wherever two armies met. That was as far as his military experience had ever taken him, and the concept of moving armies over vast distances for strategic reasons and perhaps never fighting a battle was entirely beyond his experience.

Soon the news that I had drawn a map of the great war being fought so many miles away spread to the other clans, and some of the men of the Frasers and the Campbells and the McGraws would visit our cabin, overcoming their reserve toward me since the Farqueson incident, and ask my opinion as to how matters would go. They were not especially interested in who won or lost the war, these men, holding themselves apart from the struggle. Still it was exciting to speculate on what would happen.

One of the Campbells was familiar with the Hudson Valley, having made three hunting trips through it, and, indeed, penetrated alone as far as Quebec trading furs. His view was that the British would never be able to get through. He believed that they would either be deserted or misled by the Indians and lost in the wilderness.

This Campbell, whose name was Fergus, said that he believed he would go to the Hudson Valley again and see what was happening, for he was tired of hunting and it would interest him very much to see such a big army as I had described on the march through the wilderness. He found it hard to imagine a band of more than a hundred men under arms, and, since I spoke of men in thousands, all soldiers and equipped with cannon, he thought it a shame to miss seeing such a sight. Furthermore, he added, he had never seen a cannon and would dearly like to see one and also hear one fired.

"I do not suppose," he said slyly, "that you would care to come with me, Maclaren Oge"—that was the name they called me. "The distance is near a thousand miles and it would be a matter of some danger."

"Do you think I fear danger?" I said, nettled.

"I have not heard that you settled your score with the Farqueson yet," he said. "But no doubt you are biding your time."

This was the first time the matter had been raised. There were several men present and they all looked at me—hard, impassive looks—but none of them spoke.

"The boy has seen more o' war than any of ye present, excepting myself," said the Maclaren.

"No doubt he has had a bellyful," said Fergus Campbell softly. "That may be the reason why he has not avenged himself on the Farquesons. I hear it was the canting Sassenach that saved him that day."

I got up and faced Fergus Campbell. "If the others will make room," I said, "I will make you eat your words before them or I will have your life."

"There will be no fighting between us and the Campbells," said the Maclaren of Spey. "It is forbidden."

"Well," said Fergus, "I am sorry that nothing interesting is to happen. But I am going to the Hudson Valley to see the soldiers and the cannon, and I am sorry also that the Maclaren Oge has seen so much of them that he will not come with me."

"By thunder," I cried, "I will come with you and show you I have no fear of cannon or soldiers."

"You will stay here," said the Maclaren.

"You should let him go," said the father of Fergus Campbell. "It is shameful that he has done nothing about the Farqueson. I can hardly restrain my own sons from settling the matter. If he were out of the valley the score could be evened, since he is unwilling to do anything himself."

"He is but biding his time," said the Maclaren. "He will kill the Farqueson when he is ready. He is thinking of a good trap and a good way to do it."

"I am not," I flared. "The Farqueson attacked me

when I was unarmed and that was a coward's thing to do. I will not avenge myself on a coward."

"You will avenge yourself when I tell you," said the Maclaren, "for you bear my name."

"I will not," I replied.

"Then I will avenge you," said my foster father. "And I will do it this night since the matter has been openly mentioned among my friends." And with that he picked up his rifle and went out of the cabin in which this scene had taken place. I rose to stop him, but two of the Campbells blocked my way.

"You will stay," they said with a sneer and, since they were armed and I was not, I had to remain.

Someone now produced a packet of cards, and a game was started in which I was not invited to take part. They played until dawn, and during that time I strained to hear any sound of conflict up in the mountain, but heard nothing but the wind in the big pines and three times the howling of a she wolf. Then when the dawn was well started, there was the crack of a rifle followed by another report and a scream. The card players stopped for long enough to glance at each other and then at me, and went on with their game. Perhaps half an hour afterward the Maclaren returned. He walked slowly into the hut and pushing aside the others came up to me. He pulled a hank of long yellow hair out of his belt, and I knew without even looking at it that it was the scalp of the Farqueson.

He held it up before my face and said, "That was

what you should hae done. You tainted my name and brought shame on me."

"You murdered him," I cried.

"I killed him," said the Maclaren. He laughed. "He came oot of his bothie wi' a bairn and I got them both."

"You killed a child too?" I cried.

"Aye," said the Maclaren. "A Farqueson. His woman screamed."

I looked at the others in the cabin. They were well pleased with this report.

The older Campbell filled a pannikin with rum and thrust it toward me. "You should toast your sire and his trophy," he said. "It is the custom. The heir must be the first to drink."

The others stood around waiting for me to take the pannikin, watching me in silence with hard faces. Peace of God was watching me too, anxious and pleading. Fergus had his rifle under his arm, the barrel pointed at my chest. He was grinning at me. The threat was obvious.

"Drink," said the older Campbell, pushing the pannikin at me.

"Do not touch it," said Peace of God. "It is an abomination."

"Drink," said the Campbell again, and there was a movement of weapons around me.

"Before Heaven, I will not," I cried. "You are murderers all of you. Cowards, blackguards, and murderers." I flung the pannikin aside and bolted for the door.

There was a report of a rifle and Peace of God came stumbling out behind me.

"Run for the woods," he cried.

But I was too proud to run. I heard the Maclaren shout, "Leave him tae me," and then he hailed me from the cabin.

"Turn," he cried. "Turn or I will take ye in the back."

"Shoot and be damned to you," I cried over my shoulder, but without looking around, and continued walking.

But no shot came and I gained the pines safely.

I stayed in the bottom of the valley for the remainder of the day, though Peace of God pleaded with me to set off at once and get out of the mountains to the safety of the lowlands. But then he was a stranger to the Scottish laws of hospitality—extended even toward enemies and outcasts. He did not know that for twenty-four hours I might not be killed in the valley, and that I was sure was the reason the Maclaren had not shot me when I bolted from the cabin despite his rage. Though now his enemy, I was still, under the rules of Highland hospitality, his guest. But this sanctuary would last only until dawn of the following day, when I would be hunted down like an animal.

I knew that the Maclaren would kill me. I had disowned and shamed him publicly, and so in his mind he had no other course. But meanwhile my problem was to get a rifle. Mine was in the cabin, and without one I could not hope to survive long, hunted in the wilderness. We would be five days getting to a settlement in the lowlands, and in that time we must live off game. I knew what would be happening up in the cabin. The Maclaren would be in one of his black moods and would start drinking rum, and in this he would be aided by the Campbells. It was reasonable to presume that by evening they would be fuddled, and in that state I might steal back in the dark and get a gun which was kept, in case of surprise, in the cleft of a rock a hundred yards from the cabin.

So I climbed one of the pines and made myself comfortable in the topmost branches and slept sporadically during the day to rest for the work which lay ahead at dark. Peace of God stayed at the foot, reading from his Bible most of the time, and so we stayed until it was dusk.

Just as I was about to leave my perch in the pine, the valley now being in deep shadow, I heard several cries from the direction of the Maclaren's cabin. There was then a ragged discharge of rifles and some more shouts.

I could see nothing from the top of the tree except a few faint flashes of light and got down to the ground quickly. "Let us get out of here quickly," said Peace of God, very frightened. "There is Satan's work afoot over there."

"It's the Farquesons," I said. "They've come for vengeance."

"It's no concern of yours any more," said Peace of God.

"No," I said. "It is not." Yet I could not move either toward the sounds of the fighting or away, but remained rooted where I was.

The reports of the rifles were spasmodic now, and I could imagine that the Maclaren and those of the Campbells who had stayed with him—perhaps half a dozen men—were sniping from the cabin at their attackers. Then, as I listened, there was a furore of rifle fire and silence for a while. Then through the trees I could see a glimmering of light and in the silence another rifle shot and a shout of "Maclaren Abu! Maclaren Abu!" This was followed by a shriek and then silence once more.

"Come," I said, and set off toward the cabin.

When I got to the place where the trees thinned to a little clearing, I saw that the cabin was afire and the light of the flames, very bright in the darkness of the forest, showed several bodies flung upon the ground and all blotched with blood.

Then I saw the Maclaren. He was on his knees, his hands to his head, and even as I watched he slumped slowly over to his side. I went to him and moved his hands away. There was a big bloody area on his head where his scalp had been lifted.

He opened his eyes and looked at me, and his face was full of hate.

"Ye brought the Farquesons," he said thickly. "God's curse on you."

"I did not," I protested. "I was unarmed in the forest."

"Do you swear it?" he asked.

"I do," I cried. He seemed to consider this for a moment, and then fumbled with the tara brooch but could not remove it from his jacket.

"Take it," he whispered. "The clan. . . ." I did not catch the rest of his sentence. Then he raised himself to a sitting position with a strength which I did not think he had. The red and yellow light of the fire licked about him, throwing black shadows on the ground. He looked slowly around at the bodies, which were illuminated by the flames. The blood was streaming down his face and he was wounded in several places. Yet, as I watched, appalled, he got from a sitting position to his knees and then to his feet and cried out clear and loud, "Drummossie Muir," and pitched forward dead. The cry "Drummossie Muir. Drummossie Muir" came echoing back from the mountains, as if all who had been present on that day were joining in the death shout of the last of the Maclarens.

"Come," said Peace of God. "He has gone to his Maker. We must leave." He looked around at the bodies of the fallen and then at the Maclaren and said, "'Asshur is there and all his multitude; their graves are about him, all of them slain.'"

13

Three months later I was back with the Continental Army in the Hudson Valley, having made my peace with my father. I told him plainly all that had occurred and how the Maclaren of Spey had met his death. He was not unmoved by the account, but said that such a death was inevitable for a man who had refused to move forward with the world and had sought to re-establish in the colonies the feudal system of Scotland which was dying out even in that country.

I cannot say that his welcome was very warm, and

the reason for this was that I still had with me the tara brooch. He regarded this as the passing on of the traditions of the Maclaren to myself; as a sign then that I had not completely thrown over all connection with that bloody past. Yet I could not bring myself to throw the brooch away. It was a symbol steeped in terrible deeds, no doubt. And yet there was much courage and honor of a kind attached to it. How could I take such a thing and fling it in the road or some river? My father believed that this was what should be done with it, and at times I all but agreed with him.

When we parted the problem was still unsolved and the tara brooch lay between us.

I did not return to my old company, which had been broken up, but entered Morgan's Rifle Brigade, which was a natural choice, for it consisted for the greater part of frontiersmen from Pennsylvania. And we were sent up the Hudson Valley to check the invasion of Burgoyne, who was driving toward Albany.

This was the battle of the wilderness of which my father had spoken, the opportunity to exterminate or defeat a British army with the surety that the French would then join our cause. I was still uncertain of what position he held in the government. It seemed to combine that of finance minister with the duties of a sort of civilian quartermaster general for the Continental Army and the Continental Navy. His vast experience as a prominent Boston merchant in time of peace, and his many connections with banks abroad, particularly in France, were now, I gathered, being put to their fullest use. He was a man of such station that he could secure credit on his own signature where the credit of the Continental Congress stood as nothing. I knew then that he had staked his personal fortune to the hilt to secure supplies in France. But this I found out from others, for he was most reserved with me, as I have said, and told me little of his affairs.

The fighting in the Hudson Valley was just such as suited an army of our sort. Through August we harassed Burgoyne's men as they strove to get through the wilderness to Albany. At times we cut down trees across their route—blocking whole valleys with huge timber falls. Then, as they labored to clear these away so they could bring their artillery train through, we shot at the troops at leisure. Sometimes they came after us into the deep woods, struggling through the thickets and up the wild ravines of that territory. We melted away before such sorties, then drove behind them, cutting off their return to the main body.

Once we captured six hundred Waldecker dragoons set out on just such a mission. They were unmounted —horses would have been useless to them in any case. They lumbered through the wilderness in huge cavalry boots, carrying their heavy curved swords and further laden down with muskets with whose use they were little acquainted. It was the height of midsummer and the mosquitoes swarmed in the gloom of the forest. The dragoons slapped at their faces and necks and swore and floundered in the steaming mud and lost their big boots, and we let them exhaust themselves with a ten-mile march in these conditions before surrounding them. They surrendered readily enough, glad to be out of the continuing torment of flies and heat and mud and short rations and sleepless nights and the sniping of their invisible enemy.

One of them told me that what had been worse for him was the sound of axes chopping trees ahead of them through each night.

"Always trees," he said. "One barrier cleared and then, a quarter of a mile farther on, another barrier and after that another."

Eventually Burgoyne led his whole army into a trap, and when I saw this I thought of how I had misjudged Washington. For the trap into which Burgoyne marched was one from which he could not escape. And the traps into which I had thought General Washington stumbled were ones which always provided not only a loophole, but also an opportunity to strike a blow, or at least a delaying action.

What Burgoyne did, about the middle of September, was encamp his army in a clearing beside the Hudson called Freeman's farm. With Dan Morgan's men I had been shadowing him for days, and when we saw him head for the clearing we chuckled. He hoped, no doubt, that here he could meet the Continental Army in open ground, when he was sure we would be defeated. I was perched in a tree watching the redcoats stream out of the narrow road through the thickets of the wilderness, and when they found the clearing they cheered with relief, for here was a battleground that suited them.

From below I heard a turkey gobble, which was the signal Captain Dan Morgan used to call his company together. I climbed down the tree and joined the rest of the men of the company and we were dispersed among the thickets which ringed the Freeman farm. We hadn't long to wait. The British sent out strong pickets to the end of the clearing, and we let them come to within fifty paces and then opened fire. It was Breed's Hill all over again, but this time we were not likely to run out of ammunition. Officers and men toppled to the ground and the rest ran back.

Then we made a mistake. We charged out of the clearing. The British and Hessians re-formed and came at us and drove us back. Some penetrated into the forest, but of these few returned. We had learned our lesson, which was not to fight in the open.

All day long a battle ranged around Freeman's farm. We had opened it, but it was continued and spread as more and more reinforcements came up until at last the whole area around the farm was thick with our men.

When evening came we had closed the trap. There was no way out for the British.

Then followed some weeks of what I can only describe as a combination of a siege and battle. The British dug in and put up some gun emplacements. We remained in the forest, firing at what targets offered, cutting off any parties which sortied out to reconnoiter. Meanwhile the autumn advanced and with it came the wolves. I do not know how many men were killed in the weeks of this strange siege and battle. The number ran into hundreds, and, since many fell in thickets in the forests where they could not be gotten at with ease, they were unburied. The wolves scented them and came after the dead. They grew bold, and in one night while on picket duty I shot two of them. We were careful, after the wolf packs started to gather, to let no man lie long in the wilderness wounded. But they made the nights horrible with their howling.

The end came suddenly. The British massed for an attack in which to break out of the trap. We drove at them, hurled them back, and took over some of their entrenchments. They tried to pull away to the north and were trapped again and, finding all hopeless, surrendered. When the news of Burgoyne's intention to surrender reached us, I felt for the first time that there was some hope for our cause.

The surrender itself was curiously sad. We were lined up on both sides of a glade through which the defeated army marched, having stacked their muskets. The British, in tattered red coats, were sullen and glowered at us. But the Germans were more docile and seemed almost glad that a task in which they had never really had any heart was over at last. Many of them had made pets of forest animals. One, I noted, had a little bear cub on a chain. It followed behind its master, clapping its paws and dancing a little as if very pleased at the turn of events. Another man had a squirrel sitting on his shoulder nibbling at a nut, and some of the German troops had cages with magpies and other birds in them.

After the men came their officers, for military etiquette for surrender demanded that normal forms be reversed. In victory the officers would have led the parade. In defeat they brought up the rear. They tried to look unconcerned, but it was easy to see that they were ashamed and angry and fearful that they would be jeered at. But we made no sound as they trooped by, and they seemed grateful for this.

The morning after the surrender, I was sent to the British hospital, where there were many wounded men who could not be moved. My task was to check their names against a list which had been supplied to us.

One name on the list set me wondering. It was "Colonel Sir John Pett, K.C." Could this be the same man, I wondered, who so long ago had spared the Maclaren and myself from hanging, and was he the father of the man whose portrait I had seen in Trenton wearing a stone cut in the same fashion as that of the Maclaren?

I found him in an upstairs room of the Freeman farmhouse. He had been shot through the leg and was in bed and there was a doctor attending him, for he had sufficient rank to command such service even after surrender.

"Who are you?" he demanded, as I entered, and the doctor turned around and looked at me fearfully. For answer I reached into my wallet, took out the Maclaren's brooch, and threw it to him on the bed.

He stared at it and then at me. "Where did you get this?" he asked, picking it up. "Ah," he said. "I remember now. Treegate. Peter Treegate, who was captured with the Maclaren of Spey at the siege of Boston."

He looked again at the brooch and then said, as if the thought had just occurred to him, "I presume that he is dead."

I nodded.

"Why do you bring this to me?" he demanded. Then he turned to the doctor and said, "You may leave. I wish to talk to this fellow privately."

When the doctor had left I said in answer to the question, "Because there is a man who bears your name and wears a stone cut in the same fashion. Captain Maurice Pett of the Brigade of Rifles."

"He is dead," said Sir John woodenly. "He was killed at Princeton. I have the ring here." He fumbled at the neck of his nightshirt and produced the ring which was on a piece of silk thread.

"Tell me of the Maclaren. How did he die?"

There was no reason why I should relate the story of the Maclaren's death to this man and yet I did so, and he heard me through with great interest.

"Well," he said when I had concluded. "They are together at last." I thought he referred to the ring and the brooch which he held in his hand, but, seeing the blank look on my face, he added gently, "I mean the Maclaren and his son."

"His son?" I cried.

"Yes," said Sir John. "His son. Captain Maurice Pett of the Brigade of Rifles.

"You are puzzled, eh?" he continued. "Well, you have a right to be. But reflect for a moment. For what reason do you suppose that I decided not to hang the Maclaren and yourself when you were taken at Boston? It was not mercy, I assure you—at least not mercy toward strangers. It was because I had seen this brooch of the Maclaren's with the stone in it. And I knew then that he was the father of an infant whom I had found hidden in a cave after the Battle of Culloden (Drummossie Muir) with nothing to tell who he was but this ring which was pinned to his shift."

"How did you come to find this boy?" I asked.

"I was taken to him by a witch," said Sir John.

"A witch?"

"She had every semblance of a hag," he replied. "She was clad in rags. Her hair was matted down to her waist. Her voice I recall only as a shriek and her language was unintelligible to me, for she spoke only Gaelic.

"But I see you are still puzzled, and indeed I am ahead of my story. The facts are simple. I believe you know from our meeting in Boston that I was brought down by the Maclaren of Spey in that battle in the initial charge of the highlanders which was led by his clan. My wound was a grievous one and I lost a great deal of blood. Indeed, I lay on the field for two days, as far as I can ascertain, and would, I think, have died if this hag had not come through on the evening of the second day, looking either for booty or one of her kinsmen—probably both.

"I could make sufficient noise to attract her attention. I was quite sure that she would dispatch me and indeed that was what I wished, for I was incapable of supporting my agony any longer. A wound unattended for two days and a night, and with snow falling for most of that period can become unbearable," he added.

"Well, as I say, I hoped that this hag would kill me, but instead she went away and returned after dark with a Highland pony and contrived to get me upon its back. I was then taken some distance, I do know how far, for I swooned on the way, and, when I recovered my senses, found myself in a cave somewhere in the Highlands. The woman nursed me, keeping me there for two weeks while she supplied me with food and indeed took excellent care of me.

"She never stayed in the cave with me during the day, and I was unable to talk with her because of her inability to speak English and mine to speak Gaelic. She would make her visits at night, and then only stayed long enough to dress my wound and feed me and was gone.

"At the end of two weeks, when I felt I was strong enough to leave, though still miserably crippled, I tried to thank her and by sign language explain that I must leave and return to the army. She, by sign language, gave me to understand that I must wait until the morrow. The following evening she returned with a small pony which I was plainly to ride. The pony had over its forequarters two covered panniers such as are used in the Highlands for the conveyance of goods. She opened one and showed me that there was food inside.

"Then she signaled me to leave and, since I dallied, trying to express my gratitude, she struck the pony and off it went. When I pulled the animal to a halt, the woman had gone, and there was a strange noise coming from the other pannier. I opened it and found inside an infant of no more than a few months. It was clad in a shift, and, as I have said, there was no clue to its identity but this ring with the stone set in it."

"You mean that this woman gave her baby to you—abandoned it to you? For what reason would she do that?" I cried.

Sir John smiled. "Because of the gentleman who commanded us and who was called, not without justice, Cumberland the Butcher. He planned to exterminate the Scottish clans and his extermination included infants."

"And you never saw this woman again?"

"I did indeed," said Sir John. "I saw her a week later—hanging from a gibbet on the roadside. She knew Cumberland the Butcher better than I."

"And the boy?" I asked.

"What was I to do but take him with me and keep him safe? That had been the woman's intent. She took a chance that a British officer would not kill her child if she had saved his life.

"I brought him up as my son and gave him my

name. I had no clue other than the ring to his identity. And it was only when I saw the brooch of the Maclaren that I knew who my foster son was. Plainly I could not hang his true father. And if I spared him, I could not hang you. You were his foster son, as his son was mine —as strange a turn of the cards as I have seen in the game of life."

"The Maclaren gave the brooch to me when he was dying," I said, "and I do not know what I am to do with it." I then explained how things stood between me and my father because of the brooch.

"Why do you not throw it away?" asked Sir John, looking at me keenly.

"It would not be honorable. It was given to me in trust, and yet it makes a breach between my father and me."

Sir John's next words startled me.

"I have not yet been able to go through the formality of surrender," he said. "It seems that this might be a good opportunity. Yet I should like to know to whom I am surrendering."

"What do you mean?" I asked.

"Well, am I surrendering to a member of the Continental Army of the United Colonies or to a member of the clan of the Maclaren of Spey?"

"To a member of the Continental Army," I replied.

"Excellent," said Sir John. "You will find my sword in the cupboard there. Keep it. I will keep the brooch. I fancy both will be safe with their new owners and come to no dishonor. Now if you will summon the doctor, he will bleed me a little and you no doubt have duties to attend to."

He reached out his hand and I took it.

"We have come to the final scene in the story of the battle of Drummossie Muir," he said. "Go to your father and tell him of it. He will welcome his son back."

"I believe he will," I said and left the room.

END OF THE SECOND BOOK